"The baby and I are safer here, with you."

"Do what I say, Anna." His order was more of a growl than a command.

"No." Anna shook her head vehemently. Panic seeped into her pores, clutched at her belly. "I am not going to leave you."

The rebels approached.

"If you don't, we all die." He paused no more than a heartbeat before he slid his hand possessively over hers, absorbing the softness. Too soon, he broke away. "You will go." He let his forehead fall to hers. He kissed her hard, imprinting himself on her. He forced himself to let go. But her taste stayed with him.

"And you will survive."

DONNA YOUNG

BODYGUARD CONFESSIONS

TORONTO • NEW YORK • LONDON
AMSTERDAM • PARIS • SYDNEY • HAMBURG
STOCKHOLM • ATHENS • TOKYO • MILAN • MADRID
PRAGUE • WARSAW • BUDAPEST • AUCKLAND

To my family, you are my heart

ISBN-13: 978-0-373-69283-5
ISBN-10: 0-373-69283-8

BODYGUARD CONFESSIONS

This edition published by arrangement with Harlequin Books S.A.

www.eHarlequin.com

Printed in U.S.A.

ABOUT THE AUTHOR

Donna Young, an incurable romantic, lives in beautiful Northern California with her husband and two children.

Books by Donna Young

HARLEQUIN INTRIGUE

824—BODYGUARD RESCUE
908—ENGAGING BODYGUARD
967—THE BODYGUARD CONTRACT
1016—BODYGUARD CONFESSIONS

CAST OF CHARACTERS

Anna Cambridge—The daughter of the president of the United States, whom Death has tested twice. Years before, with her 10-year-old brother's life and now, with the life of a baby prince.

Quamar Bazan Al Asadi—An ex-government operative whose faith in Allah equals his trust in a quiet step and a sharp blade—until a woman and baby need his protection. Can he place his faith and trust in love, too?

Farad Al Neyum—A thief who believes great fortune sometimes comes at a price—but when the price is a baby's life, is he still willing to pay?

Hassan Al Asada—A sheik with ambitions to rule a country. His only obstacle? A baby prince.

Zahid Al Asadi—A man with two powerful passions. His love for inflicting pain—and his hatred for Quamar Bazan Al Asadi.

Prince Rashid Al Asadi—Seven months old and ready to rule?

Chapter One

They called themselves Al Asheera. The Tribe. Revolutionaries with crimson veils that masked all but the bloodlust in the deepest black of their eyes.

Like desert locusts, they poured from the darkness, swarmed over the palace walls. Consuming. Destroying.

Some carried the poisoned spears and the tapered broadswords of their ancestors, while others—the youths—held the submachine guns and grenades of their allies.

But all were intent on one objective: to kill the Royal Family of Taer.

Quamar Bazan Al Asadi pressed his fingers to his eyes, while a litany of screams pierced the darkness around him. Their mounting pitch taunted him with their unrelenting rhythm. They were the cries of the scarcely living—souls lost somewhere between terror and death.

He thought of the servants, the guards. His cousin, King Jarek, and Jarek's wife, Saree. Their baby son, Rashid.

All dead.

Rage rose in his throat, forcing Quamar to draw short, bitter breaths through his mouth. The wind had stopped. Its strength bogged—first by the familiar stench of blood and battle, and now by the sweeter scent of hashish and cremated bodies.

A handful of Al Asheera soldiers swaggered around the palace grounds in small groups, confident in their success. Some patrolled, others stood watch from the palace's silk-draped windows while most celebrated in a drug-induced euphoria.

Quamar moved, half-crouched, to a nearby abandoned jeep. From his position, he observed the courtyard. Bodies littered the ground, strewn about like blood-spattered rag dolls among the marble statues and mosaic-tiled fountains.

Men. Women.

His gaze stopped on a dead Al Asheera soldier, who lay slumped in the jeep's passenger seat, his crimson scarf torn from his face. Quamar noted the acne that spotted his cheeks and the soft, youthful jawline that hadn't yet touched the sharp edge of a man's razor.

A boy. One who wasn't a day older than fifteen,

Quamar realized. His gaze rested on the knife tucked in the boy's belt, the sword propped under his hand. Shaving wasn't a prerequisite when it came to butchery.

The Al Asheera recruited the young. Not surprising, considering the promise of riches and rewards appealed mostly to those born poor and who hadn't suffered the horrors of war.

Frustration filled him, fed his anger. Only cowards made war against women and recruited children to kill. For that atrocity alone, Al Asheera would pay.

A dull throb started at his right temple, but Quamar ignored it. Instead, he shifted deeper into the shelter of the darkness, monitoring his surroundings. He was a big man, wide in the shoulders, with the broad, hard-boned features of the Arabic, the muscle and meat of the Italian.

Still, he was born from the desert, his body carved from its wind, sand and heat. He was a soldier by fate, not choice—a man hardened but not cruel, dangerous but not treacherous. His beliefs were his own—this by his choice—deep-rooted in faith, tradition…

And justice, Quamar thought with grim satisfaction.

More than half of the palace guards had secretly joined the Al Asheera ranks. Traitors who attacked from inside, catching those loyal to King Jarek unaware. Several had died for their betrayal, but not near enough for Quamar's liking.

A stretch of ground lay between the courtyard's rear entrance and the palace itself. A few hundred feet. Half a football field.

In the middle lay a cluster of olive trees. Just beyond, fires burned in horrific pillars, their greedy flames fed by the dead.

It was a contemptible testament from Al Asheera. Muslim law forbade cremation—considered it abhorrent—and in doing so, Al Asheera denied the people of Taer their rightful place with Allah.

In the distance, curses mingled with loud bursts of laughter. Quamar leaned forward, his gaze shifting until a circle of Al Asheera soldiers, six in all, crossed his line of sight.

At their feet lay an older man, his worn, leathered features barely distinguishable under the blood that coated his dark skin.

A servant? A soldier?

The Al Asheera bound the man's hands and stripped him down to a pair of mud-stained linen pants. Even from a distance, Quamar saw his arms were thick. Yet, where once there was strength and sinew, the muscle now slackened with old age. But it wasn't until they ripped off his turban that he saw the shock of gray hair, the deep-set brow.

Arimand.

In the flickering light, the Al Asheera soldiers dragged the old man, Jarek's Captain of the Guard, into the middle of the courtyard, then shoved him against an aged, gnarled olive tree.

Quamar edged closer, shifting toward the jeep's front tire, careful to hide from the glow of a nearby fire.

A rebel tied the rope to Arimand's secured wrists, then threw the loose end around a branch overhead. Within moments, they hoisted the guard off the ground and left him suspended mid-air with his arms stretched above, his shoulder sockets straining under his weight.

The smoke blended with the night, making the air thick and murky. For a few moments the Al Asheera poked and prodded Arimand with hot sticks and knives. But soon they tired of their game and drifted to the nearest fire for warmth.

Quamar flexed his fingers, felt the reassuring rush of blood to his hands. One against twenty was never good odds. But with every passing moment, the rebels' hashish slowed their reflexes, dulled their thoughts.

If the number equaled fifty, it would not matter. First and foremost a soldier, Quamar had come to terms with death long before.

He grabbed the boy's turban and scarf. His

home had been assaulted. His family decimated. And because of this, he waged his own personal war. Quickly, he secured the material over his head, then around his face.

A war that took no prisoners.

ANNA CAMBRIDGE STAGGERED through the underground channel. Cobwebs snared her hair, covered her face. She shoved them away. The first two or three had frightened her—along with the rats that scurried and screeched. But no more.

How long had it been since she'd escaped through the passageway? An hour? Maybe two. It seemed a lifetime.

Her steps were slow, cautious by necessity, not preference. Mud oozed between her heels and her slippers while the coarse sand clung to her pajamas, saturating both her tank top and bottoms. The cotton—useless against the cold edge of the tunnel's draft—adhered to her skin like a moist, sticky cocoon.

Her only warmth came from the baby snuggled low in a sling against her belly. Prince Rashid Al Asadi.

There had been no time to change clothes. No time to prepare. Al Asheera had laid siege too quickly.

Using her hand, she guided herself through the

pitch-black, sliding her palm over the wall's damp, jagged grooves, which cut and tore at her fingers.

The carrier acted more as a small hammock swaying with the cadence of her body. The material looped around one shoulder, then down Anna's back to her waist, allowing the baby to hang semicurled against her body.

Her free hand tightened protectively over the wide strip of woven linen. The baby lay quiet in his sling. There had been no whimper, no movement for over two hours. Alma, his nanny, had warned her he'd possibly go six. Anna frowned. He'd been drugged for his own protection and hers, long before Alma had found her. Still, Anna slipped her hand between, felt the soft beat of his heart beneath her fingers.

"Not much longer, little man," she murmured, knowing the words were more of a hope than a pledge. Alma's instructions had been desperate but insistent. Hide the baby until his father, King Jarek, or Anna's father somehow rescued them.

Then Alma had shoved a knife into her hand. *"Protect His Highness,"* she had whispered, and was gone.

No problem, Anna thought derisively. All she needed to do was find her way out of this underground maze, slip past the soldiers, over the wall, then through the Al Asheera–occupied city.

The scent of stale earth and decayed rodent slapped at her, enough to make bile rise in her throat. Her heart pounded in fear. Another dead end?

She continued along the passageway, cursing herself and the darkness. She'd made so many missteps already—wrong turns, impasses. Still, she couldn't turn back until she was sure.

A little boy—only months under ten, blond and slightly built—flashed across her mind. Her brother, Bobby, with his blue eyes wide with trust, his face pale with fear.

"I love you, Anna," he whispered against her ear, tears he'd bravely held back getting the best of him, dropping his voice to a hoarse whisper. *"Don't go. Don't leave me."* Anna pushed the memories away. But the echoes of his voice remained, riding a familiar wave of anxiety that rolled deeply within her.

She *had* left him. And her brother had died.

Cautiously, she shifted her foot forward, searching for the dead end with her toes. Anna stopped, steadying herself. The air had turned, sending a faint breeze skittering across her ankles.

A mist—more fog than light—crept across her path.

Blinking hard, she forced her eyes to adjust in the semidarkness, then used the soft haze to guide her.

At the base of the stone, no more than two feet square, lay a vent, its opening blocked by a wrought-iron grate.

Anna braced her back against the wall and slid downward, ignoring the burn of the sandstone against her bare shoulders. "Don't worry, Rashid, we're going to make it." *Or die trying*, Anna added silently. She looked down at the baby, using his warmth to ease the knots in her stomach.

With a free hand, she tugged on the grate. "Looks like they sealed it with cement," she murmured. After sitting back on her calves, she nestled the baby across her thighs. "I'm going to need both hands, handsome, so we're going to have to make you comfortable."

Outside, bushes flanked the vent, but nothing blocked the hole itself. Anna exhaled, not realizing until then that she'd held her breath.

She pulled Alma's knife from her back waistband, noting how the cold steel felt foreign beneath her fingertips.

"Here we go." After stretching across Rashid, Anna set her shoulders and began to scrape between cement and iron. Her movements were awkward and slow as she tried to keep the baby protected from bits of flying mortar. "If we're lucky, this stuff has been decaying for a hundred years." She dragged the knife around the four edges, applying pressure until her arms shook, her muscles ached.

As the daughter of the United States president, Anna had been around politics her whole life. At twenty-seven, she understood that greed undermined the rebels' strike on the royal family. Al Asheera would fail. She had to believe that.

But not before hundreds more died.

At every pass, she dug the blade farther in, scraping and jabbing, trying to separate the grate from cement. The wind picked up, drying the film of perspiration into a tight mask, making her skin itch.

A chunk of cement fell from the top of the grate. With a small cry, she dropped the knife, wedged her fingers between the metal and wall, uncaring when her nails broke. She tugged at the metal until, noiselessly, the grate fell into her hands.

Trembling, she tossed the grate to the side.

"Okay, sweetie, time to run."

Chapter Two

Arimand was dying.

Before he reached the tree, Quamar had seen the flash of the blade as the insurgent slid it below Arimand's ribs.

The rage came to Quamar, savage and swift. But death would take its time with the old man. Slow and agonizing. Just as the rebel soldier had intended.

Most of the Al Asheera drifted away, not interested in the ragged breaths of a dying man. But one remained, the one whose knife still dripped with Arimand's blood.

The guard's eyes skimmed the darkness while his feet shuffled. From cold or fear, Quamar did not know. Nor did he care. The rebel had sealed his fate the moment he had slid his blade into the old man.

Quamar shifted his weight back, his shoulders

forward, while his knife's blade lay balanced between his fingers. He waited. The ache in his head had morphed into a battery of hammers beating a cadence on his temples. Having lived with the pain for many months, Quamar pushed it away, knowing from experience he had limited time before the pounding increased.

But by then, his objective would be completed.

The guard strapped his machine gun over his shoulder and with long, thin fingers reached for a pack of cigarettes from his shirt pocket.

Quamar let loose the blade, heard the familiar *thunk* as steel impaled skull. He spared no more than a glance when the body crumpled to the ground.

After snagging the guard's machine gun, he pulled his knife free. He wiped the blade on the dead man and slipped into the darkness. Scanning the courtyard, Quamar noted that the killing had gone unnoticed. Instead, all stood watching the pillar of flames lick at the midnight sky.

"Arimand." For safety, he covered the older man's mouth with gentle fingers. The papery skin flexed beneath. "Be silent, and I will cut you down."

Arimand shook his head, forcing Quamar to release his mouth. "No, leave me. I am well beyond help now," the old guard rasped, pain etched in all the grooves of his face. "Anna Cambridge, the prince. Find them. Save them."

"Anna Cambridge?" He pictured her long, blond hair, her depthless blue eyes. It was not hard—for months the woman had haunted his dreams. "If she is here, she is dead," he said flatly. Another life to avenge.

"No. Hassan leads the Al Asheera." The dark eyes bore into Quamar. "He ordered them to hunt her down. Go now, find her and the child. Take them to your father." Arimand inhaled sharply. "Promise me," he said after a moment, his voice harsh, unyielding.

"I promise you."

Arimand nodded, then closed his eyes against the gut-wrenching pain. "You and Jarek…you both were…. If I had sons…" Arimand stopped, his eyes blinked, opened, their focus softening. "One more promise…"

Quamar nodded, stopping the words he knew hovered on Arimand's lips. Agony ripped through Quamar, forcing him to tighten his jaw. He'd spent half his childhood with this man, had grown to love him as a son would.

"Go with Allah." Quamar leaned forward and kissed the old man's lined cheek. Without a sound, he slid his own knife between Arimand's ribs and into his heart.

Arimand gasped, his heartbeat stopped beneath Quamar's hand—and with it his suffering. Quamar dropped his forehead to Arimand's. "May he keep you always."

It took most of his will, but Quamar stepped away, knowing Arimand died a warrior. With honor, dignity. Courage.

Quamar moved back toward the tree, his gaze searching for danger among the shadows. Suddenly, a burst of laughter drew his attention. His eyes narrowed on the trio of men, their interest focused past the jeep to the wall beyond.

Curious, Quamar followed their line of sight, then froze. He swore silently. If he hadn't been watching so closely, he would have missed the rustle of the bushes, the movement of shadows.

The flash of pale, blond hair.

WITH HER KNIFE IN HER side waistband, Anna hugged Rashid close and lay on her back. Her stomach churned under the baby's weight, sending the bile back to her throat. She'd come too far to lose her nerve now. Using her heels, she pushed herself headfirst through the hole and into the courtyard.

Blood pounded in her eardrums, its rhythm a fast staccato that matched the beat of her heart. Anna dragged in a long breath, then made it two, fighting off the wave of weakness that seeped into her limbs. "Just a bout of nerves," she whispered and rose to her feet. *I can do this, damn it.*

Anna forced herself to take first one step, then another. She had started the third when a hand fisted her hair and yanked her back. Anna screamed and struck out, blindly trying to gouge at the unseen features. When she found bare skin, she dug in her fingers.

A string of curse words spewed from somewhere above her head, but the hands locked tighter around the back of her neck, squeezing until the pain took her breath, forced her to her knees and into the light of the courtyard.

While another laughed, Anna bit back her cry of fear and instead concentrated on the cold steel of the knife hidden in her waistband.

From her position, she saw three of them. Identical, with their masks of red, their swords unsheathed.

War cries sounded in the distance. Soon, she knew, there would be more. She snaked her hand to her side, then gripped her knife.

No warning came. No noise, no scent, not even the ping of a bullet. One moment, a soldier held Anna, the next he froze, his features stiff with disbelief as he fell dead beside her—a knife embedded in the back of his neck.

The other two turned in unison, but neither had time to do much more. Anna saw the flash of a sword, heard the slap of steel against skin, then the screams of pain. Both men fell next to their friend. They, too, were dead.

"Get up." A large, meaty hand grabbed her arm and hauled her to her feet, jarring her knife free. With a thud it hit the ground. Her captor's eyes strayed to the blade, then back to her.

"Pick up your weapon," the man ordered, leaving his own in the dead soldier. "Now." While his hand remained tight on her arm, he allowed her to stoop and grab the knife. For a moment she hesitated, gripping the handle.

"Do not be a fool." His words were clipped, his tone annoyed. The man was a mountain of gloom towering over her with the crimson scarf draping most of his face. At five-six, her head came midway to his chest. His black robes caught in the wind and flitted against her in a devil's dance, setting off a shiver of trepidation. By sheer willpower, she forced her fear back and stood her ground.

"I am your only way out, Anna Cambridge."

The Al Asheera closed in, fanning out in a half circle and forcing the giant to shift his back to the tunnel's vent.

"For now," she answered, her chin raised, but

the fear grew at his mention of her name. Quickly, she put the blade in her waistband, but left her fingers hovering over its handle.

Her action, while subtle, didn't go unnoticed. Anna heard the grunt of surprise, then caught the giant's gaze. His dark irises flickered with something—approval, maybe—before he shuttered the emotion closed.

Anna counted more than a dozen Al Asheera, some with swords raised high, others with guns leveled.

A spray of bullets peppered the ground in front of the rebels, kicking up dirt and forcing them to stop within feet of Anna and the giant. So close she caught the sour scent of their bodies, felt their excitement ripple through the air.

Her skin crawled with revulsion. Anna cradled Rashid with her free arm, for the hundredth time grateful he slept.

"Come any closer and die." Her captor's voice was pitched low, while the words he spoke were French. The language second only to Arabic in Taer.

The nearest soldier, older than most, with a scar that reached from his temple to nose, hesitated only slightly before he stepped toward the baby.

Her captor's rifle discharged. Anna stifled a

scream as Scar Face jerked, then stumbled while his hands grasped at his chest. Men shifted out of the way, let Scar Face fall, ignored him as he writhed on the ground in agony.

"Anyone else wish to come forward?"

"You cannot kill us all," came the reply. A chorus of grunts followed his remarks.

"Move one more inch and you will be the second to die, Zahid," her captor responded.

Anna gasped, recognizing the name. Zahid Al Asadi, cousin to King Jarek Al Asadi of Taer. The betrayal knifed through her.

Zahid salaamed, his black eyes flickering first over Anna, then Rashid. "We meet again, Miss Cambridge." Anna's gaze shifted toward the middle of the half circle until it rested on the man who spoke. Dressed as the rest with black robes and his red headgear, he wasn't large in size. A good head beneath most of the men, with shorter legs and a fairly broad upper body. So large in fact it made him look top-heavy.

Before Anna could answer, Zahid turned toward the stranger. "And you are?"

The giant shook next to her. But when she spared a quick glance, she saw the set of his shoulders, the narrowed eyes and knew it wasn't fear that caused him to vibrate, but rage. "I am a man holding an M4 assault rifle," the giant rasped.

Anna heard the click of the weapon, saw the Al Asheera shift back before he continued. "The bullets will cut most of you down in three seconds. Starting with you, Zahid." Without hesitation he grabbed Anna by the scruff of the neck and brought her forward.

"You, in turn, will be firing at me and this woman." When she cursed him and struggled, he tightened his grip. "Be quiet," he snapped, his gaze not leaving the mob. "This is the daughter of the president of the United States. In her arms she holds Prince Rashid Al Asadi. What do you think will happen when they die in the cross fire?"

Zahid's stance shifted, but not before Anna noticed the tight fists at his sides. "All right." Zahid's words were slick with oil, his tone cajoling. "You have made your point."

The stranger released Anna. "As of this moment, they are my property. But I am more than willing to…sell them for a price."

"If you care about our cause, you—"

"I have no allegiance to your crusade. I care only about their worth in ransom."

Surprised, Anna glanced up. So the man wasn't Al Asheera. He might work for another faction of terrorists, but it did not matter at this point. Escaping from one man would be much easier than escaping from a dozen.

"We will escort you into the palace," Zahid responded. "And I will personally see you are rewarded."

The man's laugh was no different than his words, low and raspy. He nudged Anna behind him. The temptation to run prodded her, but she managed to quiet the urge. If she ran now, they would have no alternative but to shoot.

"I will find my own way to the palace." Steadily, they backed away, the giant's body now shielding her and the baby, his gun never wavering on the mob that followed. "Tell your father, Zahid, I will be in contact."

The giant swung his machine gun toward the jeep and let go a burst of gunfire. An explosion shattered the air, the jeep burned in a ball of fire, putting a wall of flames between them and the soldiers.

Two of the rebels screamed in rage and rushed through the fire, but their robes caught the sparks and ignited. Some tried to save them, while others cried out and ran from the blaze.

The giant fired into the remaining Al Asheera even as he pushed her back toward the vent.

"Go through," he ordered. "Now."

Zahid grabbed a man, using him as human shield. Bullets struck the man's chest. Still Zahid held him.

"Go!" When the giant's weapon jammed, he threw it to the ground.

Anna hit the dirt, clutching Rashid. She slid back through the open vent, losing her slippers in the process.

For a big man, the giant moved with an eerie swiftness. She hadn't risen to her feet before he stood beside her. Once again looming over her.

Desperate, Anna kicked the back of his knee and sent him crashing to the ground. Without waiting she started running, dragging her hand along the wall to keep her balance. His curses filled the air, but she didn't let the viciousness deter her. Adrenaline pumped through her system. Her chest clenched, the panic swelled, threatening to collapse her already shaky legs.

While the walls were brick, the ground was still dirt. Sharp pebbles bit into her feet, causing her to stumble more than once, but sheer willpower kept her from crying out.

Suddenly, she was grabbed and pushed toward the wall. The giant's body, hard and immovable, covered her and Rashid.

Behind them an explosion hit the air, the tunnel shuddered and the earth trembled. The wall collapsed in a roar of rocks and dirt.

Before she could gather her thoughts, he jerked away and grabbed her arm. "Grenades. Go!"

They ran through the obscurity—him leading the way with unnerving accuracy.

Only after long minutes did he stop.

A cloak of darkness surrounded them, its air clogged with dust and smoke. Anna tried to draw in a breath, ease the weight of fear in her chest but there wasn't enough oxygen in the air.

"Shallow breaths." The whispered order brushed her ear while his body pressed closer to her, its hard lines, the breadth of chest defined against her naked shoulders. A shiver of—what?—anticipation, fear—ran through her.

"We are safe for the moment. I detonated the grenades to stop them."

"You're sure?" She struggled to find his outline in the pitch-black, unnerved by the detached voice floating above her head.

"Yes, I am sure," he answered with derision. "We are under the city. Far enough away to rest a moment. But only a moment."

"Good." She snagged her knife, jabbed the point into his stomach, backing him up a step. "Now, if you don't let me go, I'll kill you."

Chapter Three

"You are being foolish," came the irritated reply. Anna couldn't see him, but she felt him, his body vibrating with barely suppressed anger. "Without my help, you risk yourself and the baby."

"I have no reason to trust you or anyone else." Another jab. This time the giant hissed. "So back off."

"I am Quamar Bazan, Miss Cambridge. Do you remember me?"

"Quamar—" Her jaw snapped shut.

Of course she recognized the name. Quamar Bazan had worked as an agent with Labyrinth, a black ops organization connected with her father. One she hadn't found out about until recently. "I'm supposed to take your word for that? When I can't see your face?" She jabbed at him again for emphasis.

Quamar quickly grew impatient. "I can prove

it, if you will allow me." It was one thing to distrust him, quite another to keep poking at him with her blade. "But I must reach into my pocket."

"All right. But slowly or you're going to lose some fingers."

Quamar heard the tremor in her voice, then the bite as she clamped down her fear. She was terrified, yet she maintained her stance.

She has courage, he admitted silently, almost reluctantly, as he pulled his light out of his pocket. And she would need it to see her through the next few hours.

He thumbed the switch, igniting the lighter. The dim fire cast an amber glow between them.

Beautiful, he thought, before he could stop himself. Even the streaks of mud over her brow and across the soft curve of her cheek didn't detract. She studied him with blue eyes that were big and set apart, wide enough to balance the feminine cut of her chin, soften its stubborn edge. Her lips were full and wide with the balance toward top-heavy. Enough to entice most men, he imagined, to taste.

Slowly, she lowered her knife.

"Quamar." There was no relief in her voice or fear. Just anger.

And his name trembled with it.

Since he'd expected the relief, her anger surprised him. But it shouldn't have. He had been critically wounded a year ago while on an assignment to protect Anna's grandmother from an assassin. And he had failed.

He, more than most, understood that past transgressions were never forgotten.

"You could have told me earlier." She brushed her hair out of her face. Mud-splattered, it spilled down her back in a stream of blond tresses that curled between her shoulder blades. Thick enough to bury a man's hand under its weight.

When his fingers itched to do the same, he tightened them on the lighter. "When was I supposed to tell you?"

"Outside, where I could've seen you."

He growled, a harsh grinding of his vocal chords. "If I had, I would be dead. And you would be Zahid's prisoner," he snapped with more abruptness than intended, resenting her anger and the connotation behind both. "Or dead, too."

"I could have killed you," she said, her tone matching his. With jerky motions, she sheathed her knife in her waistband.

So, he thought, that is where the anger came from. Her fear of almost hurting him.

Not from their past.

"No, you could not have," Quamar responded, his mind back on their position. It had been years since he'd explored the tunnels. Erosion could have weakened the passages for all he knew.

"In the future, do not warn your enemy before you strike," he said, deepening the tone to soothe, allowing his words to settle before he pushed the blade away. "Strike to kill."

"You're damn lucky I didn't."

"It was not luck," Quamar answered with forced equanimity. Quamar was a patient man by nature. The desert life killed those who weren't. But somehow with Anna Cambridge the edge of his patience became slippery, making it difficult to hold on to.

"Where did you come from, Quamar?"

"The desert," he answered abruptly.

"I see," she said, frustration underlining her response. But when he wasn't willing to give more information, she asked, "Where in the desert?"

"Where I was before does not matter. What matters is we are here and cannot stay." His eyes ran over hers, checking her for injuries. "Rashid did not cry over the explosion." He pulled open the sling, allowing the light to shine on the boy. "Is he dead?"

Anna felt his body tighten, the only give of emotion.

"Only sleeping," she said, sensing rather than seeing him relax at her explanation. "His nanny drugged him for his own protection."

"I understand," he said, and let his hand drop. "So, where do we go from here?"

"We get you both out of Taer safely." He motioned toward the baby. "And to do so, you will need to trust me, Miss Cambridge."

"Trust you? When just minutes ago you were talking ransom to Zahid? I've only met you once, and you were unconscious at the time. That isn't a foundation for trust." The harshness was gone, but wariness kept her eyes wide, the bow of her lips tight and pale.

After her grandmother's murder, Anna had visited Quamar at the hospital. He remembered the cool flutter of her fingers on his hand. The brush of a kiss against his lips—an act of forgiveness that he did not deserve.

Over the past months, he had thought of that one kiss a thousand times. "I was not unconscious," Quamar remarked. "Tell me now, do you *ever* do what you are told? Or do it without argument?"

"Do you?"

This one wasn't startled easily. Cool, collected. But he had surprised her. He saw the flush rise over the pale cheeks.

"Yes, I do," he lied without qualm before his eyes moved to the baby.

"Quamar," Anna said with impatience. "I have promised to see Rashid to safety. I do not make promises I can't keep. So I will trust you. *Only* because I have no other choice. But do not expect me to follow you blindly. Not with Rashid's life at stake."

Her jaw tightened, hardening the stubborn lines. Still, the trepidation was there in the shadows of her eyes.

Something pulled at him, deep from his belly. A familiar tug, one he'd felt before and many times since.

The threads of fate.

Quamar pushed the feeling away. "Agreed." He shut off the lighter and pocketed it.

Catching her elbow in a viselike grip, he urged her forward. "We have wasted enough time. We must go."

They traveled in silence, occasionally stopping to listen and wait. The air turned dank and the chill seeped through the soles of her feet, making her bones ache, her body shiver. The sling bit into her neck and shoulders. Without thinking, she shifted the baby, relieving some of the pressure.

"How is he?"

He must have sensed her movement. Instinctively, Anna's arm tightened over the baby. "He hasn't woken yet." Her hand went to Rashid's nose, felt the tickle of his breath against her skin. "But his breathing is even."

"You have done well protecting him," Quamar acknowledged. But before Anna could digest the compliment, or the warmth it invoked, he asked, "What are you doing here, Miss Cambridge?"

"Running for my life, it seems."

"In Taer," he corrected, but she heard the sigh in his voice. "What are you doing here in Taer?"

Without warning, his hand slid down her arm and snagged her hand. The meaty palm engulfed hers, warmed her chilled fingers.

"Saree invited me. We went to college together. I have known her for years. Since my father was getting ready to negotiate with Jarek over Taer's new oil discovery, I figured I would visit for a few days. See Rashid. Take in the sights." Anna didn't comment on why, because this was not the time to release inner demons. "Sort of a diplomatic vacation."

Suddenly, Quamar turned a sharp corner, pointing them in a different path. Which direction, she wasn't sure, having lost all bearing hours before.

She paused, wondering. "How do you know these tunnels so well?"

"Jarek and I are cousins. As well as Zahid. We played in them as children."

"Cousins? You tried to kill your own cousin?"

"Yes." Quamar's answer was matter-of-fact. No explanations. No justifications.

"You would have killed him if I hadn't been there."

"Yes." It was a rhetorical statement, but Quamar answered anyway.

"Your family reunions must be real fun," Anna muttered.

"They will send men to cover the entrances. We need to be gone before."

"They?"

"Hassan and Zahid."

"Hassan? Zahid's father?" Anna asked, unable to stop the disbelief in her voice. "You're saying your uncle is behind the attack?"

"He will benefit the most. But he had help. A traitor among Jarek's ranks. Hassan could not have disabled the palace security from the outside, not long enough for the attack. Only someone from inside could have made them vulnerable."

"How many people had access to the codes?"

"Half a dozen. Maybe less."

"Quamar, a good portion of the palace soldiers turned on Jarek and his men," Anna said. She'd seen it herself. Men killed with swords or bullets in their back.

"Something Jarek would never have expected," Quamar acknowledged. "Jarek innately believed most people of Taer loved the country, honored it as much as he did. Were loyal to his father and the crown. It was a flaw I had warned him about. And now it has cost him his life."

In the few short days she had known Jarek, she had come to respect him and his views. He epitomized royalty. Not just in looks, although his features were defined in a mixture of the sharp angles and broad planes of his ancestors. But more. Jarek wore his royal heritage like one wore an expensive suit—custom-tailored to fit the long, thin lines of his frame. And he had worn that heritage well.

"We must hurry. A short distance from here is a fork in the tunnel that leads out into the city," Quamar said, his voice grim.

"And once we escape to the city? What are we going to do?"

"Survive."

Chapter Four

Farad Al'Neyum was a man driven. Not by honor or faith.

But greed.

Above him, he could hear the distant rap of a machine gun, the bellows of the soldiers as they hunted their enemies. Farad grunted with disgust. All fools who believed in an empty cause—to rid the people of Taer of antitraditionalists.

A cause brandished like a sword from a wealthy man who wanted no more than power and further riches.

Riches he had yet to see himself, Farad admitted while he pushed against the sewer grate above his head. With caution born from years on the street, he poked out his head and scanned the alleyway surrounding him.

Empty. Pleased, he set his gun out on the cement and levered himself out of the drain hole.

He could taste the rot of sewage, feel the sludge stick to his skin, soak into his robes. But the stench didn't bother him. Hadn't in years. In fact, he'd become accustomed to the more fetid scents of the city. It wasn't every man who owned his kingdom, even if it was the sewers of Taer. For even the rich needed somewhere to wash their garbage away.

Farad was a small man. In truth, no taller than the hind leg of a camel, and rather plain with a sharp nose, pointed ears and gaps between his teeth.

But he wasn't one to dwell on his lot in life. He placed the grate once again over the drain.

With his size came an above-average intelligence—a quality lacking in the local law enforcement. One he used to his advantage.

Quickly, he moved down a nearby alley. Every so often he stopped and listened. In the distance sporadic gunfire sounded, but not close enough to be dangerous.

Feeling better, he stretched the tight muscles in his back. It had been a long evening, but a profitable one. With a smile, he lifted the leather pouch at his waist, tested its weight, heard the jingle of coins. Jewelry and money he had found on the dead. Paltry, considering. Not enough to last through the week.

His gaze skimmed over the rooftops of the *souq*—Taer's marketplace—until it rested on the golden crest of the palace in the distance, still lit in all its glory. A glut of treasure waited beyond the long line of its columns and archways, protected just underneath the rise of its domes.

Praise Allah, he thought with derision.

Even an above-average thief didn't risk the loss of one's hands or head for palace riches. Especially during a revolution. Too many people would be suffering before the dawn broke over the horizon again.

No one ever cared about a thief's lot in life. And Farad wouldn't lose any sleep over others' woes. He sighed and scratched his armpit, wondering if he'd picked up a flea or two from bedding down with the camels the night before.

Tonight, at least, he'd have money for a mat on a warm floor. And some hot mint tea.

Abruptly, a rock bounced, its sharp rap echoing off the cobblestone. Farad froze mid-scratch. He grabbed his rifle from the ground and edged to the corner of the building.

Blond-white hair caught in the yellow wash of the streetlamp. A woman adjusted the bundle in front of her, her fingers fumbling in her haste. Suddenly, she glanced over her shoulder and Farad caught the full image of her face.

Her features—delicate, with the traditional lines of the Westerners—were now pinched with fear, her body covered only in flimsy attire, her feet bare.

Leaving his rifle, Farad slid along the pavement, careful to stay down within the shadows of the street's gutters. Deftly, he shuffled forward on elbows and knees, stopping twenty feet from the woman. Excitement set the hairs on his neck straight. Anna Cambridge. He had seen her many times on television, in the newspapers.

Within seconds, a man—a true Goliath—caught her arm and pulled her into the shadows. The man's warrior stance, his panther-like quietness, seemed familiar. Instinctively, Farad shifted farther into the sewer's trench.

Patience, he reminded himself.

The couple slipped into a nearby alley. Farad followed them even while excitement bubbled within, forcing him to resist the urge to clap with pleasure.

The giant posed a problem, but not so big a problem Farad couldn't resolve it profitably.

After all, he had waited a lifetime to find the treasure beyond all treasures. And now, it stood less than twenty feet away.

His thin lips twisted with satisfaction.

Praise Allah.

THE CITY OF TAER WAS NO MORE than a tangled network of narrowed lanes and tightly compressed buildings.

"Where are we going?" Anna whispered.

Intermittent streetlamps glowed dully throughout the streets. Each block contained pastel-colored shops with apartments of white stone squeezed sporadically in between.

They had stopped, cloaked by shadows and a doorway. The pungent smell of cumin and stale grease permeated the air, telling Quamar he should have chosen something other than a bistro for rest.

The pain in his head increased, a chisel scraping between skin and skull. He closed his eyes for a moment, hoping for a little respite, but the heavy scent of spices antagonized the ache. He thought about the pills in his pocket, knowing they'd bring temporary relief. But the relief would come at a price. Slower reflexes, impaired judgment.

"We are going to a friend's," Quamar answered, the censor obvious in his tone. He scanned the area, searching the shadows for danger.

"Your friend or mine?" Anna muttered under her breath, but not low enough for Quamar to miss.

"Mine." His eyes flicked over her, daring her to make another comment.

Anna frowned, her hand patting the baby's

back for courage. "Why not the airport? Or maybe steal a jeep?" She kept her words low, doing a damn good job at imitating his censured tone.

"The airport will be guarded and all the roads shut down. A vehicle will only be a hindrance where we are going. Do not worry, Miss Cambridge. I will get you to safety. But first, you need clothes."

Her chin lifted at the insult. "I'm not worried," she responded in a harsh whisper. "Just uninformed."

She didn't bother hiding her annoyance. And somehow she managed to look down her nose at him, even though he towered over her by a good foot.

Maybe later, that trick would impress him. Right now it only irritated him.

Quamar had spent most of his life keeping his thoughts and emotions hidden. But it took most of his control to bite back the snarl that rose in his throat.

He understood her fear, better than she did. The more information she had, the more she believed she controlled the situation. Uninformed, as she put it, kept her balanced on a precipice of fear. He didn't have time to alleviate her fears now. First, he needed to get the two of them off the street.

But even terrified, the woman wasn't easy to intimidate.

And she was definitely a woman. The sling covered most of her chest and abdomen, but not enough to disguise the fact that Anna Cambridge had soft, feminine curves and a waist no bigger than the span of his hands. Desire bit at him with sharp, jagged teeth, annoying him further. "If you must know, we are going to my father's camp. But first we need a satellite phone. And supplies."

Sirens sounded—announcements blared from loud speakers warning the citizens to stay in their homes or risk being shot.

He grabbed her hand, engulfing it once again in his own. "Come." His command was clipped, leaving no room for argument while he pulled her along. "And be quiet."

Her immediate gasp told him she'd been insulted, but she didn't respond. Instead, she tried to yank her hand away. He caught her wrist, this time in a firmer grip.

The rumble of engines grew in the distance. "Trucks," Quamar murmured. "More soldiers to patrol the streets. We must hurry."

He picked up his pace, pleased when Anna did the same and did so quietly. After several minutes, Quamar stopped near an apartment building. Larger than most, it stood at the end of the street—

ten floors of modern steel and glass towering over the shops in the *souq*.

An Al Asheera soldier sat on the front stoop, his scarf lowered to allow a cigarette to hang from his mouth. His rifle rested nearby, propped against the door.

"Wait here," Quamar murmured, his lips brushing against the soft shell of her ear. When she shivered against him, his muscles tightened in response. Biting back a curse, he jerked away.

Quamar snagged a rock from the ground. He tossed it once in his hand, testing its weight, then threw it at a nearby garbage can. The soldier shot to his feet, his eyes darting back and forth. With hesitant steps, the Al Asheera approached.

Quamar waited with his back tight against the wall, the corner only inches from his face.

The man stepped past, his rifle raised. Quamar knocked the weapon away, heard it clatter on the street. He grabbed the man's head and twisted. The sound of bone cracking split the air.

Anna cringed, fighting back the bile that rose to her throat. Quamar snagged the man's turban, handed it to her along with the rifle. "Hold this." He picked up the body and tossed it toward the back of the alleyway as if it were little more than garbage.

After he placed the dead man's turban on his

head, the scarf over his face, he grabbed back the rifle. Hesitating, his eyes bore into hers. "Are you going to faint?"

"I don't faint," she responded, swallowing back more bile. Her legs wobbled for a few moments, but she stiffened her knees to stop their shaking. She'd be damned if she gave in to the weakness.

She expected to see anger but she saw nothing but a dark void in the giant's irises. No emotion. No regret.

Like most weapons, Quamar was clear, concise, cold.

And, God help her, right now she was grateful for it.

He led her through a lobby, decorated tastefully, if not minimally, with scarlet drapes, Persian rugs and the occasional potted plant.

Automatically, Anna moved toward the elevator only to be pulled short by a hand on her shoulder. "Stairs," Quamar murmured close to her ear.

With quiet feet they climbed each flight of pristine-white steps—the vague scent of ammonia still clinging to its tiles.

Quamar stopped them mid-step. A door creaked somewhere beneath. Someone coughed and Anna's nerves snapped and sizzled, like live wires beneath her skin. The slap of shoes echoed throughout the stairway only to fade seconds later when another door banged open.

Perspiration beaded at her temples while her muscles remained tight. Only when he tugged her forward again did she dare breathe.

When they reached the seventh floor, Quamar stopped and cracked open the door. A bright light pierced through the semi-dark stairway. Anna squinted until her eyes adjusted.

Quamar studied the hallway with care, noting one Al Asheera at the end of the corridor. The man sat cross-legged on the floor, his back against the wall and a rifle across his lap.

His eyes were closed.

A decoy?

A dozen doors stood between them, six on each side. Each door potentially hiding more Al Asheera.

Quamar studied the doors, looking for any jarred open or for fresh foot tracks by their thresholds.

Anna shifted behind him but otherwise remained silent. The woman was astute and learned quickly. That simple fact might save her life, he thought grimly.

In the stream of light, Quamar placed his forefinger to his lips, then pointed to Anna's feet. "Stay," he mouthed.

One short nod told him she understood, but her frown told him, once again, she wasn't pleased about it.

Soundlessly, Quamar crept down the hall, picking up the light scent of polish, the stronger scent of sweat and tobacco.

The guard's eyes flickered, then opened. But when he caught sight of Quamar, he scrambled to his feet rather than firing his rifle. A fatal mistake.

Quamar's knife hit, sinking into the guard's forehead, his surprised features a death mask as he slumped to the floor.

Expertly, the giant searched the man. Finding nothing, he shoved the body into a nearby utility closet, grabbed his knife and the rifle, then waved Anna forward.

Quamar tapped on the door.

Seconds ticked by. Quamar tapped again.

"Who is it?"

Quamar spoke too low for Anna to hear, but after a few words, the door opened.

A woman, no more than thirty, petite with feathered black hair just past her shoulders, waved them in.

"Quamar." Relief underlined his name.

Quamar placed a finger to her lips, gave her one of the rifles. With silent steps, he made his way through the apartment, searching the adjoining rooms. A few moments later, he returned and motioned Anna into the apartment.

Tentatively, she glanced around. Luxurious by any standard, the apartment still managed a homey appearance. Muted, jeweled colors of sapphire, emerald and ruby draped the walls, covered the floors. A balanced blend of patterns and solids, mixed with the darker mahogany of the furniture, did more than relax—it soothed the senses.

"Your mother will be out in a moment," Quamar said, before placing both rifles on a nearby dining table. "I caught her by surprise."

For the first time, Anna took a good look at her rescuer.

Oh, he was tall, she'd known that. Even in the hospital bed, the blankets and bandages hadn't been able to hide the height of the man. But they certainly hid the massive strength beneath.

The romantic in her recognized his stance as that of a warrior—taut, tense but poised. To protect, to rescue those he stood guard over—those he deemed defenseless. Her. Rashid.

Broad shoulders and bulging muscles were well defined under the flow of his black robe. Bare-chested, his rich, bronzed skin glistened with sweat and golden undertones where his robe parted into a V, framing the rigid abdominal muscles. He wore his dark pants loose and low on lean hips. But the cotton did little to conceal the firm, tight-muscled thighs beneath.

The woman in her took him in with one, slow stroke of her eye, recognizing instantly the attraction that fluttered in her stomach.

He'd taken off the turban, giving her an unobstructed view of his face. Dark eyebrows framed onyx eyes and long, thick lashes. Their arch, concealed now with a frown, she imagined appeared with a vengeance once his humor surfaced. If he had one.

He kept his head and face clean-shaven, adding a smooth texture to otherwise masculine features. His jaw was chiseled with a slight cleft in his chin—cut from the same stone that carved his high cheekbones, the straight slant of his nose.

His mouth, beautifully sculptured from the Greek gods—hard and sexy, with just enough give to hint at something softer beneath.

"Miss Cambridge, are you all right?"

Startled, Anna looked up to catch Quamar studying her. The black deepened enough to indicate he'd been watching her awhile.

"I'm sorry." Heat flushed her cheeks. "Yes, I'm all right."

"How about you, Quamar?" the woman asked, frowning as she glanced between the couple.

"I am fine, Sandra." Quamar's half smile only

brought a raised eyebrow from his friend. He bent down and kissed the woman's lips. A brief kiss, one of reassurance. Not passion.

Sandra's leather-brown irises narrowed with concern. "I'll just make sure you all are. If you don't mind." She walked across the room and grabbed a large black bag.

"Anna, this is Doctor Sandra Haddad," Quamar stated when the woman returned. "Her father, Omar, is the physician to the royal family. Sandra is Taer's coroner."

"My father? Is he…" Sandra paused, unable to go further.

"The Al Asheera won't harm your father, Sandra." An older woman stepped from a nearby hallway. Her accent placed her as British. Older by at least thirty years, her skin showed little of her age. She was trim and petite, barely passing Anna's shoulder. A glance from mother to daughter showed they had the same hairline, the same brown eyes. "He is too valuable. There is need of him." And, Anna noted, the same stubborn line in their brow.

The woman paused long enough to caress the top of the baby's head.

When Anna took an instinctive step back, the older woman smiled. "I'm Elizabeth Haddad. A friend."

Before Anna could answer, Elizabeth addressed Quamar. "Prince Rashid is not safe here. Nor is Miss Cambridge."

"The baby, he has slept through everything?" Sandra asked, already reaching for her flashlight.

"Yes," Anna answered, trying to keep her concern at a minimum. "His nanny drugged him."

"How long has he been out?" Sandra asked, checking the baby's pupils.

"Over three hours now." Anna's arm tightened, protecting.

"Not the best way, but it served its purpose." Sandra opened the sling and snagged the bottle from the baby's lap. She unscrewed the lid and smelled. "*Passiflora Incarnata*. Not harmful but concentrated. When he wakes, he's not going to wake happy. She had to give him quite a bit to keep him out this long. He might even have a slight headache, not all that different to a hangover."

"But he'll be fine?" Anna asked.

"Yes. He's fine." Sandra stroked Rashid's forehead.

"But you aren't." Elizabeth's gaze took in Anna's mud-caked clothes, her bare feet. "You've been injured."

With a frown, Anna followed Elizabeth's gaze to the floor. For the first time, she noticed the blood-smeared footprints behind her.

"You are bleeding?" Quamar noticed the red marks on the floor. "Where are your shoes?"

"Slippers. I lost them running in the tunnel. Going back for them would've slowed us down."

Quamar swore. He opened the door, gave Anna a hard stare, then disappeared into the hallway.

"What was that about?"

Anna sighed. "That's his 'Don't you dare move while I'm gone' look."

"Really?" Elizabeth mused. "I've known Quamar since he was a child, and I've never seen more than a 'I'm not going to let my feelings show' look."

Anna would have laughed, but she couldn't figure out if Elizabeth was being serious or not.

Before she could ask, Quamar stepped back in and shut the door. "The rug is red, which covered your marks. But the stairs are a different matter. One that worked in our favor. I cleaned them down to the fifth floor."

He glanced at Sandra. "Who placed the guard outside your door?"

"Hassan," Elizabeth replied with derision. "At least that's what the guard said. Under the ruse of protecting us, of course. He is keeping us safe in order to force Omar to help his soldiers."

"The guard is dead. We have very little time before he is discovered. I had no choice, he saw me. But I took him down to the fifth floor also."

Sandra nodded toward Anna's feet. "We'll clean up our floors, too."

"All the communication lines are down." Quamar walked to the bay window, eased the curtain barely an inch and studied the street. "I am taking you to my father's camp." He turned back to the women. "But first I need your satellite phone, Sandra."

"I don't have it," Sandra replied. "It's at my office. I only use it for my field research."

"Then we go to your office," Quamar stated. "Right now, I need you both to get ready."

"No," Sandra said. "I have a better chance of retrieving the phone if I stay. If people are injured or dead, they are going to need me and I am going to need my office. Just tell me who to call."

"You are not staying."

"Yes, Quamar, we are. If they come to our door, I will tell them the guard never reported to us. The worst they will do is assign another man," Elizabeth argued. "I'm not leaving my husband."

"Quamar," Sandra said. "Hassan won't harm us. He needs us too much."

Quamar looked at her for a moment. "All right, I will give you the number to an associate. And a message. Memorize both."

Sandra brought him a pen and paper. Quickly, he wrote the information. "Roman D'Amato. Talk to no one else," Quamar added.

Anna didn't recognize the name. "Will your man be able to contact my father?"

"Yes."

"Tell him to say 'no worries' when he reaches my father."

Quamar's eyebrow arched. "A code?"

"A confirmation."

"When were you going to tell me about this?"

"It's not like I didn't mention it on purpose, Quamar," Anna retorted. "I've been a little preoccupied."

Anna turned to Sandra. "When I refused having a Secret Service detail, my father devised this alternative," she explained. "It will confirm you are a friend."

Sandra nodded. "That's easy enough."

"Tell us, Quamar, how many have died?" Elizabeth asked.

"Many Taerians. Not near enough of the Al Asheera," Quamar commented with a chilling finality.

"Your responsibility is to the prince and now, Miss Cambridge. Not revenge, Quamar," Elizabeth advised.

Quamar's features hardened. "First one, then the other."

Chapter Five

"Yes. It is always that way, isn't it?" Elizabeth commented.

Quamar's features hadn't changed, but the set of his jaw moved, tightened ever so slightly.

Watching, Anna understood. Quamar Bazan was enraged. He just did a damn good job hiding it.

He didn't want to be here. He didn't want the responsibility of her or the prince. What he wanted was to destroy the Al Asheera. To avenge the dead. His family.

But wasn't Rashid his family, too?

"Sandra, you take care of Quamar while I tend to Miss Cambridge."

"Please call me Anna." But as she made the request, Anna's eyes flickered over Quamar. Fate had tossed them together, taking the decision of survival away from both of them. Prince Rashid came first.

"She stays with me, Elizabeth. They both do." Quamar crossed his arms over his chest.

"I have been a doctor's wife for thirty-five years and have learned something during that time. She won't come to any harm. We'll just be down the hall, Quamar," Elizabeth said, the hard line of her statement leaving no chance for argument. "I will keep the door open."

Elizabeth led her down the hallway to the last bedroom. "I have met your mother, Anna. You are very much like her." Elizabeth's lips tilted ever so slightly, but her voice softened. "Smart, diplomatic. But be careful, don't underestimate Quamar. Now—" she walked to the adjoining bathroom "—let me help you and the prince get cleaned up. We do not have much time. And we've wasted too much already with talk."

"The airports will be controlled, so will all the main roads," Quamar stated grimly from behind. Anna jumped. The man moved like a jungle cat.

"See what I mean?" Elizabeth murmured to Anna. "He does like his way."

"We'll be crossing the Sahara, Elizabeth. To my father's camp."

"And the baby?"

"He is Taer. He will be fine," Elizabeth said. "Quamar will make sure."

Sandra entered the room with her medical bag.

She caught Anna's eye and smiled. "Looks like we've moved to the bedroom also."

Anna took one look at Quamar and shook her head. "You're worse than the Secret Service."

Quamar merely lifted an eyebrow over the insult.

"Let me have a look at you, Quamar."

Without argument, Quamar sat on the corner of the bed.

"How bad is the headache?" Sandra asked, before flashing the light at his right eye.

"Bearable."

"Do you have your pills?"

"Yes. But it does not matter."

"No. I guess it doesn't," Sandra responded somberly.

Sandra's light slid from one eye to the next. "You need rest. The headache will only worsen."

Quamar caught her hand, pulled it away from his face. "I am fine."

Sandra said nothing, only held his look for a long moment. "Do not worry," he added.

"I can't help it," Sandra retorted softly, then tugged her hand free. "I'm a doctor. It's my job." Her voice hardened on the last word. "I just wish I was better at it."

"Sandra—"

"Just take your medicine when you can, okay?"

"Okay." Quamar's smile, while brief, took his features from attractive to heart-stopping handsome.

Little pinpricks of warning skittered down Anna's spine. She groaned silently.

Featherlight fingers touched Anna's arm. "Come, Anna." Elizabeth glanced at her daughter, then to the giant. "I'm assuming that you will allow Anna to close the bathroom door?"

Anna automatically held the prince tighter. "Rashid can stay with me," she said, not realizing until she spoke that her statement was almost identical to Quamar's earlier one.

"You might just understand Quamar better than I thought," Elizabeth responded.

"Put Rashid on the bed, Anna," Quamar ordered. "I will watch him."

Anna started to protest, but knew it was a waste of time.

"You can change his diaper, then, too."

Quamar grunted. But whether it was a yes or no, she couldn't decide.

She pulled Rashid out of the sling that held him close, then placed him down in the middle of the bed. At six months, his hair had grown into a thick mop of pitch-black. She touched it with trembling fingers.

This time, Elizabeth placed her hand on Anna's

shoulder lightly—a mother's comforting touch. "He'll be fine."

Without waiting for Anna to respond, Elizabeth eyed Quamar. "You don't look like you need clothes, which is a blessing. Omar is shorter than you by a few inches. And leaner. His robes wouldn't fit." Elizabeth glanced at her daughter. "Sandra, find Anna some clothes from Jamaal's room." She turned back to Anna. "He is my son. Studying also to be a doctor in the United States. He is built smaller—like my family—so his clothes should fit you better."

"Men's clothes?" Anna asked.

Quamar answered for Elizabeth. "They will be looking for a woman with a baby. Not two men."

Elizabeth paused, considering. "Of course, we're going to have to hide your figure."

Anna felt Quamar's gaze run over her, and she looked down. Her body wasn't svelte, but curvy with a small waist that flared into rounded hips and thighs.

Now with the sling off, the pajamas stuck to her like a second skin. She wore no bra under the tank top, something she did only at night. Her breasts were too large to go braless any other time. Heat rose in her face.

"And hide your hair." Elizabeth ran a hand over Anna's blond locks. "Maybe cut the length shorter so you appear more masculine."

"No," Quamar answered, abruptly enough to raise the older woman's eyebrows. "The turban will cover her head. If it comes off, they will see it is blond and it won't matter whether it is short or long. It cannot be helped."

"Very well," Elizabeth agreed. "Her eyes are blue. That cannot be hidden."

"It also cannot be helped," Anna stated wryly. "Maybe a pair of sunglasses?"

"For both of you, I think," Sandra concurred. "Sunglasses will help with your headache, Quamar."

Quamar nodded. "We'll need water. And some food."

"Only some?" Anna asked.

"You must travel light. It takes water to digest food. In the desert, your body will need the water for other purposes."

"You also need milk," Sandra added. "I have a few cans, but you'll have to find more somewhere." She frowned. "We have no bottles."

"I have the one his nanny gave me. And a few cloth diapers with pins. They're in the sling, under the baby."

"Alma?"

"Dead," Quamar said flatly. "They are all dead."

"Alma acted as a decoy. She took a roll pillow and wrapped it in Rashid's blanket," Anna explained. "After she slipped out, she made sure the soldiers saw her so I could escape. I didn't realize what she was doing until it was too late."

"Come, Anna," Elizabeth urged quietly, her hand already on the bathroom door. "We'll take care of the prince after. While you're getting dressed, I'll change him."

She grabbed a washcloth and soap. "Sit on the side of the tub and lift your foot, Anna. The sooner you get washed up, the safer we'll all be."

THE STREETS WERE NO LESS daunting before sunrise. The acid scent of gunpowder hung heavy in the air, but where it once was alone, it now mingled with the more fetid smells of animal fur, urine and feces.

Dressed in black linen and robes, Anna once again followed Quamar through the maze of streets. On his back, he carried a pack with provisions.

With Elizabeth's help, she had bound her breasts tightly to her chest, then tied the loose ends of the long, cotton strip around her middle. The padding gave her more of a masculine line, visible when the wind kicked up and plastered her robes to her body. Masking the baby beneath her robes would take a little more effort.

Quamar deftly maneuvered between alleyways, around corners, through abandoned buildings. Each step silent, each deliberate. Anna studied Quamar's movements, learned, tried to duplicate.

Soon their surroundings changed. White-washed apartments and cozy street cafés gave way to shanties and warehouses.

"Where are we?" she whispered when they stopped by a corral containing almost two dozen camels.

"In one of the poorest areas of Taer. Here we will be less conspicuous." Quamar guided her to a hobbled camel. He paused, then continued on. Anna knew better than to voice other questions swirling through her mind. Now wasn't the time.

"We must be quiet," he whispered. "We don't want to be discovered here. I do not have enough ammunition to get into a gunfight. And we need milk for the baby." It wasn't until the fourth camel that he stopped. Using his knife, he cut through the rope that bound the camel.

Anna felt a slight twitch at her belly. It was her only warning. Suddenly, Rashid arched his back, pushing against her. She braced herself a second before the cry wrenched through the silence of the street. Anna lifted the robe up and over her shoulder. "Shh, baby. It's okay."

Rashid's brown eyes locked onto hers, his face scrunched into a fierce frown and he let out a howl.

Chapter Six

White-hot pain ripped through Jarek Al Asadi from chest to back, jerking him awake. Bone ground against bone, while cartilage and muscle cramped beyond agony.

He fought for oxygen, but with each breath came more pain. From a cracked rib, maybe two. Quickly, he assessed his injuries. The ribs would be a hindrance but certainly didn't incapacitate him. Blood coated his tongue, dripped from his lips—the source being either his broken nose or the split inside his cheek. He blinked, forcing his vision to focus through the sweat and grit. One eye was completely swollen shut. From the same kick that had broken his nose, he imagined.

The air was pitch-black and fouled by the scent of blood and perspiration. Jarek blinked, waiting for the shadows to form into decipherable patterns.

Steel bit into his wrists and cold brick scraped at his skin. They had stripped him down to nothing, leaving him naked in the chill of the room. He didn't need to see his prison to know he'd been locked in an old cell beneath the palace.

He lifted his arms, heard the chink of chains, felt the pull of their weight. He tugged once to be sure they'd chained him to the wall. The length reached a nearby grate-covered drain—a foot-wide pipe in the floor—presumably there for him to relieve himself.

The door opened with a clank and a thud. A light flashed into his face, causing Jarek to grimace with discomfort.

"I see you've awakened, Your Highness."

Jarek stiffened at the voice, recognizing it instantly. "Where is my family, Hassan? Where are Saree and Rashid?"

"You will see Saree soon. Rashid is another matter."

"What have you done with him?" Fear had Jarek pulling at his chains.

"I have done nothing. Anna Cambridge has escaped with him. You'll be pleased to know that Alma was loyal right up to the moment she died." Hassan flashed the light about the prison, until it settled on Jarek.

Alma dead? She'd been a surrogate mother, his

nanny. Grief scraped at his insides. Rashid was safe. And Anna. But Saree? "The president isn't going to sit around while you chase after his daughter."

The light came back to Jarek's face, but not before it caught Hassan in its frame. Every feature on the older man's face was long and leather-creased—his nose, cheekbones, even his forehead. It was almost as if someone had grabbed his long, white beard and pulled down, distorting the features like a children's cartoon character.

"No, he wouldn't." Hassan's features sharpened with cruelty, a jackal before its kill. "That is why I am on a tight schedule." Hassan held up his hand when Jarek snorted in disgust. "I want to know where Bari's encampment is. I know my brother tells you the route his caravan takes, just in case an emergency arises. And I would classify this as a dire emergency."

"Go to hell."

"Before you make a rash decision, I think you need to be reminded what's at stake."

A woman's scream pierced the air. Saree?

With sweat-slick hands, Jarek gripped the steel behind him, yanking it, ignoring the fresh flow of blood over his hands. He bared his teeth. "You bastard."

Hassan clapped his hands together twice. And

almost immediately a guard approached with a woman, dragging her by her hair.

"Jarek!" A sob escaped Saree as she struggled to her feet. Her black hair, once in a sleek bun, lay in tangled strands around her face. Her nightgown, ripped on the shoulder and neckline, hung loosely over her arms and chest. "You are alive. I thought… I thought…"

When she tried to step forward, the guard jerked her back by her hair. Saree screamed and grabbed at his hands. With fists and feet she struck out at the guard.

"Enough!" Hassan's order snapped through the room. "If you want Jarek to live, you'll stop this nonsense."

"No!" But Saree stopped, her chest heaving with gulps of air.

Hassan grabbed her by her chin and forced her head back. He placed a knife by her neck.

"I could kill her now, Jarek," Hassan purred before he slid the knife up to Saree's cheek. Blood trickled from the corner of her mouth. He smeared it with his blade. "Or maybe just damage her a little."

A sob caught in his wife's chest.

Jarek's throat contracted painfully, making his words gritty. "If you harm her, I will kill you."

"You still don't understand that I have won,

Jarek. It is no longer a question of harming anyone. It is a question of when and where and how much pain." Hassan sighed, then let go of Saree's chin.

"Maybe you just need time. And some motivation."

Hassan grabbed Saree's hair and brought her face to his. "Put her in the room next door." He glanced at the guard. "Then make her scream."

RASHID HOWLED, HIS ARMS waving in angry protest.

"Hurry," Quamar yelled. Sirens sounded, grew louder until they drowned out the rumble of an additional truck filled with soldiers. "Someone reported us."

Quamar swore, then let the camel go. He hit another's backside and another's until all awoke in the corral.

Anna reached into the sling and pulled out the full bottle of milk Sandra had prepared. When she tried to put it in the baby's mouth, he pushed it away. Rashid shrieked, but Anna ignored him for the moment. "We're leaving the camel?" she asked.

"We have no choice. We need to move quickly." Quamar cut the hobble ropes on the nearest camels, letting the animals run loose in the yard. Some of them growled while others snorted, upset at being roused from their sleep.

"Use the camels for cover and follow me." Within a scant second, Quamar took in the surroundings. Mostly warehouses, they were easy enough to get lost in.

Headlights flashed through the buildings, announcing the arrival of two more trucks. Bullets shattered a window behind Quamar, raining shards of glass across his back.

"Go!" He fired his rifle, catching two of the Al Asheera in mid-jump from the tailgate of the truck. Both tumbled to the ground, their bodies still.

A locked wrought-iron gate separated the camels and warehouse. Quamar pointed his rifle and pulled the trigger. The lock exploded. He shoved open the gate and pushed Anna through.

Bullets strafed the ground. Anna screamed, stumbled, then went down. Pain exploded through her kneecaps. Quamar clamped down on her arm, half lifting her, half pulling her with him.

"Keep going!" He was taking a risk they wouldn't kill her, using the bullets instead to force her to stop.

Methodically, he returned their fire, grunting when more than a few soldiers fell dead. "Inside!"

Quamar followed Anna into the warehouse yard. His eyes already focused on the metal shanty a few yards away. He kicked in the door and shoved her inside.

It was an office, not much bigger than a toll booth and held little more than a swivel chair and metal desk. But it did have a back door.

"Get down."

Without hesitation, Anna crouched in the corner, her body curled around the baby. Rashid arched his back, his cheeks glistening with drool and tears. His cries turned to hoarse sobs.

Gunfire shattered the windows, pelted the walls above their heads. Anna choked a scream back, not wanting to add to the baby's fears with her own.

"I can give you a head start. Take the rear door. Once you get out back, go around the warehouse. Stay close to the walls. In the shadows it will be hard for them to follow you. It is your only chance."

"Me? What about you?" Anna tempted Rashid with the bottle, moving the nipple against his lips. This time he latched on greedily, taking gulps in between small hiccups.

Quamar peered out of the window. Al Asheera poured from two trucks, an army of men carrying guns and grenades.

"They need to think you are here with me. When I draw their fire, you run for the cemetery. Do you know where that is?"

"Yes, toward the palace, past the mosque, beyond the olive groves," Anna whispered, her voice hesitant. "But it's the wrong way."

"They will think you've headed for the airstrip or the desert. It will take them time to figure out you haven't."

"You want me to wait for you there, right?"

"No." Quamar crouched next to her, pulling her close until mere inches separated their faces. The rancid scent of gunpowder hung between them. "Save Rashid. Understand?" *Save yourself,* he demanded silently.

A tremble rippled through her and into him. The urge to gather her close overwhelmed him. "Take the pack." Swiftly, he maneuvered out of the straps. "When you think it's safe, double back and head for the desert. Find a caravan. Most are loyal to my father. When Sandra makes her call, either your father or mine will find you."

A surge of panic hit Anna between the shoulders. Quamar wouldn't survive, and they both knew it.

Chapter Seven

"No." Anna shook her head vehemently. Panic seeped into her pores, clutched at her belly. "I'm not going. We're safer here, with you."

"Do what I say, Anna." His order was more of a growl than a command.

"No, if I go you will die—"

"If you do not, we all die." He paused no more than a heartbeat before he slid his hand around her neck, pulled her to him. His mouth settled possessively over hers, absorbing the softness. Too soon, he broke away. "You will go." He let his forehead fall to hers. "You will survive. Do you hear me?"

She nodded with a quick jerk of her chin.

"Say it, Anna," he urged, this time keeping his words gentle. "I have to hear it, *Habbibi*."

"Yes," she whispered.

He kissed her hard again, imprinting himself on her. "Keep the baby quiet or all will be lost." He forced himself to let her go. But her taste stayed with him. "Wait for my signal to run."

Rashid whimpered. Anna gathered him, held him under her chin, using the bond to stop her arms from trembling. "Shh, honey." Without thought, she covered her hand over his ear, pressed the other to her chest. She started humming a tuneless song, keeping the tone low, soothing.

Another grenade exploded, closer than the last. Quamar tensed, ready to attack. He shifted toward the window and peered out. In the darkness, he saw the silhouette of a man, one that seemed familiar, on the roof across the alleyway. Without warning, the man switched positions, swathing his face in the light of the moon.

"Master Quamar! It is me, Farad!" Flashes of lightening spewed from his weapon toward the Al Asheera. "I'm here to help you!"

Before Quamar could respond, gunfire burst from the street, pelting the roof wall. The little man ducked.

Quamar swore. What was the thief up to?

"Who is Farad?" Anna asked.

"An old acquaintance. One I thought was dead."

"Run. Save the woman," Farad yelled, already pulling another grenade from his belt. Some soldiers dove for cover, others returned fire, targeting the little man.

"Maybe our luck has changed." Quamar shoved his last clip into the automatic rifle.

"What do you mean?"

"Since we have acquired help, I am going with you." He grabbed her wrist and pulled Anna out into the smoke-filled street. "Farad is keeping the Al Asheera pinned."

"But your friend will die."

"Farad is not my friend. He is a thief." A nearby truck exploded. Men screamed in high-pitched agony. "But it seems even a thief has his moments. We will not waste his. Follow me."

"You're going to leave him?"

Quamar's features hardened. "My job is to save you and the prince. I intend to do just that." He tugged her across the shack and through the back into the adjoining alleyway.

Darkness surrounded them, but Quamar seemed unaffected. Without misstep he led them out of the city, his dark skin blending into the black shadows of the trees and the desert sands beyond.

SMOKE ROLLED OVER the rooftop in thick waves, obscuring the streets below. Farad blinked the sting from his eyes. His fate lay in the timing. Cries of the wounded echoed off concrete roofs. Below, car doors slammed, men yelled orders as more Al Asheera jumped into the fray.

Farad cursed the fact he'd thrown his last grenade to catch Quamar's attention. Grenades he had gotten from a dead soldier.

Quickly, he sprayed the area with gunfire, then dropped to the ground, leaving his back against the wall. Using his knees and elbows he crawled across the rooftop. The other side of the building had a gutter that ran down to the street. If he shimmied down the metal tubing, once at the bottom, he could slip into the sewers unnoticed.

Suddenly, the little hairs on the back of his neck stood at attention. He scrambled faster, ignoring the sharp scrape of concrete against his skin.

When his fingertips closed over the rooftop's concrete wall, he grinned, then shifted for leverage.

A pair of fists gripped his hair and jerked him back on his feet. Before he could cry out, steel jabbed at his throat. Farad froze.

"Some of those men you killed were my friends." A squat man who appeared as round as he was tall, held a small, curved knife against the thief's throat. "You are willing to die for your friends?"

"They are not my friends," Farad whispered. "I work for Zahid."

"Well, then. Isn't this your lucky day," the soldier taunted.

Farad's eyes widened when Zahid Al Asadi stepped from the rooftop door. With a few angry strides, he reached Farad and jerked him up off his feet. "Who are you?"

"He says he works for you, Master Zahid," the soldier responded with a smirk.

"Then how come I have never seen you before, little man?"

"My name is Farad, Master Zahid." Farad fell to his knees, keeping his eyes down, his nose against the ground. "A humble thief, and your loyal servant."

Zahid laughed viciously. "And you expect me to believe that after you helped the man and woman escape?"

"I did not want your men to kill them by mistake. I know how valuable the woman is. And the prince."

"Or you wanted to capture them yourself for ransom. Like the man with them."

That was exactly what Farad had in mind. Get close enough to the man and woman, kill the man and take the woman back to the palace. If the Al Asheera had captured them, Farad would have lost his chance at the treasure.

"Ransom? Why would your cousin ransom the woman?"

Zahid went still. "My cousin?" He jerked Farad up from the ground until they were nose to nose. Hatred burned in the onyx of Zahid's eyes.

"Master Quamar." Farad deliberately kept his voice contrite. "Is he not your cousin?"

"And how do you know Quamar?"

"I've had…dealings…with him before. Years ago. In the market." Farad had tried picking his pocket and almost lost his hand in the process.

"Really, then you are friends?" Zahid quirked his eyebrow.

"More like acquaintances," Farad managed. He found it was safer to bend the truth than to tell an outright lie.

"And after you helped them escape, just how were you going to catch up with them?"

"They are headed for the desert but are moving slowly because of the baby." Farad looked down at the ground, trying to appear humble. "I do not wish to brag, but I am exceptionally good at tracking."

Zahid released Farad and crossed his arms. "You are sure they are headed for the desert?"

"I heard Master Quamar earlier. He told the woman he was taking her to Sheik Bari's encampment."

"Did he say where this camp was?"

"No."

Zahid stared at the thief a long moment. "What is that on your belt?"

"My purse… It holds only meager possessions—"

Suddenly, Zahid yanked Farad's purse from the little man's belt and opened it up. Grunting, he tossed it to the soldier and then issued the man an order. Farad strained to hear his command but couldn't.

When the soldier left, Zahid turned back to Farad. "Okay, thief," Zahid mused. "How would you like to earn your fortune in a much easier way?"

THE SUN ROSE OVER the flat horizon, blurring the line between sand and sky. The intermittent ebb and swirl of the desert wind did not cool but incited, like small bursts of air from a furnace. Each powerful enough to sandblast any exposed skin with dust and grit.

Anna trudged next to Quamar in silence, more out of necessity than choice. The adrenaline had long since waned from her system. Sweat stung under her breasts and at her armpits, where the binding rubbed her raw. But her discomfort came second to their safety. Rashid's safety.

While the heat and movement lulled Rashid back to sleep, her bindings pressed in on her. Nausea rolled in waves through her belly, while her chest tightened against the flow of oxygen.

Minutes melted into hours, yards stretched into miles, giving her no concept of time or distance. The sun-baked terrain burned through Anna's leather boots, leaving her drained, her throat parched.

"We will rest here for a few hours. It would do us more harm than good to travel during the heat of the afternoon."

Anna stopped and was suddenly so weary, her legs trembled with fatigue. Nothing but scrub and rocks surrounded them. Since she had no experience at desert survival, she took Quamar at his word.

"Why did you kiss me?" She hadn't meant to ask that question, didn't even know where it came from. The fatigue, maybe.

Quamar studied her for a long minute. She found herself holding her breath and immediately let it go, wishing she'd waited to ask. Or not asked at all.

Scarf and sunglasses covered his face, leaving her no hint of his feelings. Not that the granite features beneath would have anyway, she thought with derision.

Her only consolation—she was similarly disguised.

"To stop any further discussions," Quamar replied. But instead of dismissing her, like she expected, his stance widened, almost as if he was readying for battle.

"Well, I guess it worked," she said softly, trying to swallow the unexpected lump that lingered at the base of her throat. What had she wanted, a vow of undying love?

No.

"And the reason you didn't talk to me in the hospital?"

"Considering the circumstances, I felt it was for the best." This time he did turn away, essentially dismissing her.

Carefully, to hide the unexpected hurt that came with his words, she eased Rashid out of his sling. Keeping him under her robes and out of the sun's glare, she brought him up against her shoulder, grimacing when her muscles flexed in protest.

"How safe are we?" she asked, intentionally changing the subject. Quamar searched the ground around a nearby boulder.

"Safe enough for now. Sit over here. There are no snakes or scorpions." Quamar nodded toward the shadows of some rocks, which offered a small portion of shade. "Stay away from the others. There might be creatures trying to find a cool spot, too."

"Don't worry." Anna took a shaky step forward, and suddenly Quamar's hand was under her elbow, helping her to the largest boulder.

"When's the last time you ate?"

Anna had to stop and think. When was the last time? So much had happened. "Yesterday morning."

Anna sat, her spine ramrod straight in order to breathe with her chest bound. Quamar lifted an eyebrow at her rigidness, but chose not to comment. Instead, he crouched down in front of her and grabbed the canteen from the backpack. "Here, drink this," Quamar ordered, but this time his voice held a low, husky timbre that gentled his arrogance.

He untwisted the cap, leaving it dangling on the canister and pulled the scarf from her face. Without waiting for her to shift the baby so she had a free hand, his fingers circled the back of her neck. When she grimaced from stiffness, he automatically massaged her tired muscles. Anna let out a small sigh of pleasure.

Quamar lifted the canteen to her lips and eased her head back. "Small sips."

The water was tepid, but sweet, instantly soothing the dryness in her throat. Greedily, her body drank until too soon, he pulled the canteen away. "You can have more later, after you eat. Too much will make you sick."

He pulled his scarf from his face and tilted

back, taking a long pull off the canteen. A sheen of perspiration glistened over his skin, drawing her gaze to his throat. As he swallowed, she followed the movement of the thick, corded muscles down his neck as they flexed and bunched.

A flutter rose through her stomach, then bumped at her heart. She wanted to quit staring, she really did. But the muscles bunched once more, fascinating her.

Anna had never seen a man make drinking water look so sexy.

He lowered the canteen, slowly, staring at her through his sunglasses. Desire thickened the air between them, sucking out the oxygen.

Without realizing the consequences, Anna licked the dryness from her lips, drawing his eyes down. She didn't see them, but she knew all the same when the little hairs on the back of her neck stood at attention.

She did it again.

"Stop it, Anna." Quamar's voice was low, raspy, but he didn't move. But he wanted to, she could tell. His muscles tightened, his jaw hardened. Hell, he looked like a snarling black panther ready to pounce.

Now wouldn't that be interesting?

Chapter Eight

The fluttering knocked against Anna's ribs, setting off a spasm of anticipation that rose through her chest.

She cleared her throat, breaking the tension. "Well..." Her mind blanked. "Huh," she added inanely. For the first time in her life, she had a panther by its tail and didn't know what the hell to do about it.

Being attracted to Quamar was more than stupid, it was dangerous. And she had enough danger going on in her life right now.

Without a word, he rose in one swift, easy movement, reminding her again of that panther. But Anna noticed him flex his hand into a fist at his side. Somehow the gesture made her feel better, took away some of the hurt his words caused, even though a mutual attraction added another deadly edge to their trip. At least she wasn't the only one affected.

"We are going to stick to small water holes, far off the normal paths," Quamar said, his voice cool, the control back in place. "We will stay away from the oasis and wells where most people gather. It will be a difficult trip, but my father's camp is only three days away."

Anna absorbed his words, his tone, used them to calm her system, to get back her footing with their circumstances. "Is there any other way of getting hold of him?"

"My father's communication is limited to the caravans. They can go as many as six months without seeing another human being." Quamar grabbed the backpack and opened the top flap. "Jarek always knows where my father is. It was something my father insisted on so if Jarek needed him, Arimand could send one of his men to deliver the message." He rummaged around for a second, then pulled out a handful of dates and a few chunks of oat bread.

Anna remembered Jarek's Captain of the Guard. An older man with a quick mind, and the manners of a gentleman. "Surely Arimand would have—"

"Arimand is dead." Quamar waited this time for her to shift the baby, then handed her a few dates. "And even if he had not died, he would not have sent anyone. Not unless he knew for sure they were loyal to Jarek."

Anna paused, recognizing the harshness behind Quamar's demeanor. He had lost almost everyone he considered family. She, more than most, understood the emptiness, the frustration, the self-deprecation that haunted those left behind to grieve.

"Quamar, I'm sorry about Arimand. Saree had told me how much he meant to you and Jarek."

When he didn't answer, she didn't press him. Instead, Anna took a bite of dried fruit, but the sweetness did little for her appetite. She forced herself to chew, then swallow.

"Arimand died because of who he was," Quamar explained. "What he believed in. Most who remain loyal will face the same fate at Hassan's hands."

Pain ripped through Quamar's head from temple to temple, but he welcomed the headache this time, using it to diffuse the desire that stirred his blood, caused the pressure between his legs.

Damn it, he should have known better when he offered the canteen. He fought the urge to pull off her turban, run his fingers through her hair. Instead, he tried to appease his desire by massaging her neck, but her sigh, the soft mewing in the back of her throat, caught him unaware. Pushed his attraction to the surface.

"Quamar?" Anna nibbled on a fig with white, even teeth. Need whipped through Quamar, forcing him once again to struggle for control. "What did you mean when you said your uncle wasn't the only one behind the takeover?"

Quamar studied the horizon, silently thanking Anna for her help. The thought of Hassan's treachery cooled Quamar's desire quicker than any cold shower would have. "Hassan is clever enough to realize the ramifications of the rebellion, and he, as the next in line to the throne, would be the most suspected. He would need a powerful ally to help alleviate any suspicion or at least support his hostile claim to the throne."

"Who has that kind of power?"

"Another country. Someone in the private business sector with enough clout to forestall any rumors," Quamar replied grimly. "The possibilities are endless. Ever since Taer discovered oil beneath their land this past year, the corporate vultures have been circling." Quamar finished eating and offered bread to Anna.

She shook her head and instead brushed the crumbs from her fingertips. "Jarek had plans to meet with my father."

"Yes, he believed it was time to westernize Taer without compromising its traditionalism." Quamar put the food back into the pack. "Your father was the one person Jarek felt could help him accomplish that goal."

"He's right. My father could help him." Robert Cambridge had beliefs. Most of them stemmed from integrity, loyalty, love. Some of the many reasons Anna admired her father.

"I agree."

"Surely, others must have escaped as we have."

"It is hard to say. If they did, it would be to the desert or a bordering country. Either way, it would be hard to survive such a trip." Quamar snagged his knife from his boot and walked over to the nearby brush. With quick, decisive movement, he cut two long sticks.

"Now that Jarek is dead, who is next in line?"

"Rashid." Quamar whittled the ends of the wood into points, then tested one against his finger before carving off more.

"But he's just a baby."

Quamar paused and looked at her. "A Senior Regent will be established temporarily to run Taer until Rashid is old enough to take over."

"Hassan?"

"Hassan will not live long enough," Quamar vowed. Then he stabbed the two sticks into the earth, first one then the other, placing them several feet apart.

He took off his robe, tied the ends to the sticks,

making a primitive lean-to. For the first time, Anna saw he wore a black gauzelike shirt beneath, unbuttoned. The shirt flapped open in the wind, revealing the hard form beneath.

"Take a nap. We have a few hours before the heat dies off, and we can continue. Now is the time to gain some more strength." He scraped away the hot sand until he found the cooler earth beneath.

"Are you?"

"I will be fine," Quamar assured her. "We are still too close to the city for both of us to rest."

Anna settled her and Rashid under the lean-to. Once on her side, she opened her robe over the ground, then laid Rashid down on the cloth.

She took off her sunglasses and placed them above her head, then glanced his way. "Thank you, Quamar. For saving us."

"I have not saved you yet."

"That's true," she murmured and closed her eyes, trying to hide her wayward smile, "so I guess I'll take it back."

"SO, ZAHID, YOU ARE telling me that this stranger escaped and took Anna Cambridge and Prince Rashid with him?"

Hassan Al Asadi pushed back the gold silk curtain and gazed out of the sculpted window to the layers of city lights below. It had been over four years since he'd planned this coupe.

The satisfaction rolled through him. The Royal Palace stood above—a towering mixture of marble, iron and mortar with high stone walls and imposing domes. All cold, hard materials that belied the power within. But now it was his. And soon Taer would be his also.

"He didn't escape. I let him go." Zahid yanked off his scarf and left it hanging from his turban.

"Do you have any idea who this stranger is?" Hassan asked the question with his own barely concealed anger.

"Quamar."

Surprised, Hassan glanced over his shoulder. "You know this for sure?"

"Yes."

"It's been years since his last return. Why now?"

"Maybe someone informed Quamar of our plans? Maybe that's why he has come. To be the hero once again."

Of course, there had been no love lost between the three cousins. Only Jarek and Quamar had truly bonded, more because of temperament than age, Hassan admitted. A fact that his own son resented. Although, at thirty-eight, both Jarek and Quamar were almost ten years older than Zahid.

"Then it was a mistake to let him go," Hassan stated. He returned to his desk, a large Edwardian piece made of dark mahogany. One of the few pieces the British had left behind when they'd released Taer from their rule a hundred years before. "We've worked too hard to fail now."

"We won't fail, Father."

Hassan poured himself some tea. "You realize this ordeal could've ended tonight except for your ineptness."

"If I had captured Quamar, we would never have had a chance to find Bari's encampment," Zahid argued, before his tone turned silky. "Unless Jarek proved cooperative."

"No, he did not."

"Then tracking Bari could take days, even weeks. We can't afford that much time. Once Bari finds out about the rebellion, he will seek help from his allies. Including President Cambridge. Or the prime minister of England."

Zahid crossed the royal office. Its stone pillars and black checkered tile were all but hidden under a menagerie of dead animal skins, skulls and heads, along with various weapons from years past. A trophy room.

His lips tilted in a derisive grin. "I've managed to find someone who will lead us first to Quamar and Miss Cambridge, then to Quamar's father.

Once they arrive at Bari's camp, we attack. And Bari will die." Zahid stepped to the fireplace and reached for the coiled bullwhip that hung over the mantelpiece.

"And so must Quamar, don't forget," Hassan added before taking a sip of his tea. The sweet, mint taste soothed, taking the edge off his anger.

"I'll tell you what I haven't forgotten." The long leather unwound, and its tail slithered to the floor with a distinct hiss. He checked the handle for balance. "I haven't forgotten that as a bastard, Quamar still shares our name." With a quick flick of his wrist he aimed the whip at a nearby deer's head and snapped off the tip of its ear.

"Quamar's relationship to the Al Asadi name does not change your status to the crown," Hassan responded, his words clipped. While Hassan preferred being a master swordsman, Zahid had studied the art of the whips—a hobby Hassan had allowed, but on occasion regretted. Usually, when Zahid's control slipped, some unsuspecting woman or child was scarred. "But his allegiance to Jarek may cause us problems."

"Bari abdicated his throne for that Italian whore, and yet he and his son have loyal followers," Zahid commented.

"Nomads. Herders. Farmers. Use your intelligence, not your emotions. Bari no longer has access to soldiers." Hassan dismissed Zahid's comment with a wave of his hand.

"It wouldn't matter whether he did or not. I will kill Bari and his son. Then I will capture the American woman and Prince Rashid," Zahid said before recoiling the whip.

Hassan leaned back in his chair, propped his elbows on the arms and interlaced his fingers—a common gesture, Zahid knew, when his father was frustrated or displeased. And right now, he was both.

"As chief advisor to the king, I can stall the world for only a few days. No more than four." Hassan's eyes were large and droopy, almost hidden behind the rectangle glasses of a scholar. They seemed comical until one looked into his cold, black irises. "After that, the word will get out. The prince must be returned here before we fail. Robert Cambridge might be the president of the United States, but he is a father first. A father who has already lost one child."

"Have we decided to give her back? After I'm through with her of course." Zahid tapped the whip against his thigh, enjoying the thought of spending some quality time with the president's daughter.

"Once you find her," Hassan pointed out with derision, "we'll decide."

"And Jarek? Is he no longer an option?" Zahid sat on the corner of his father's desk and pulled out a cigar from Jarek's humidor. "Is he dead?"

"No, but as I said earlier, he's proving to be quite stubborn."

"He said nothing?"

"The guard said he didn't move a muscle. He sat in the next cell with his head against the wall and just listened to that poor woman scream." Hassan remembered Jarek's features—hard as granite, inhuman. "For three hours she begged and he did not react."

Zahid glanced up, catching the disbelief in his father's tone, the hint of reluctant admiration.

Jealousy clutched at him, its talons sharp enough to anger. "I have some free time," Zahid said easily enough, then studied the tip of his cigar. "Maybe I should take a…stab…at trying to convince him?"

Hassan hesitated, knowing the risk was high that his son might get carried away. But did it matter? "All right, but do not kill him. Not yet."

"And if he leaves me no choice?"

Hassan opened his palms in acceptance. "Then he leaves you no choice."

Smiling, Zahid salaamed to his father and without another word left the office, the whip still in hand.

Hassan sighed, then hit the button on his desktop intercom. "You heard."

"Yes," came the voice from the phone, the tone hoarse more from anger than not. "And if Zahid fails?"

"He has two chances. He will succeed."

"For your sake, he had better."

Chapter Nine

A high-pitched shriek ripped through the air, jarring Quamar. In one movement he was up on his feet with gun in hand.

The baby rolled over on his stomach and made spit bubbles until they dripped on his little fingers. He squealed again in delight.

Gently, Quamar lifted the boy and looked him squarely in the eyes. Rashid grabbed Quamar's lips and squeezed, then laughed when Quamar pulled away grimacing. "So you are finally done with sleeping?"

With a chuckle, Quamar snuggled the baby against his chest. Within seconds, Rashid pulled on Quamar's shirt. Using the cloth for leverage, the baby tried to climb.

Quamar tickled his belly, the baby laughed and grabbed for his finger. "You are going to be a strong king." Rashid yanked Quamar's finger toward his mouth as drool glistened over his lower lip.

"I do not know what I am going to do with you, but I vow I will protect you." Quamar wiggled his finger.

Rashid smiled, revealing pink toothless gums. He let go of Quamar and instead tried to grab the nearest of Quamar's shirt buttons.

"And we will protect you," Anna answered, her voice still husky from sleep. Quamar glanced over, stunned. Sometime during her slumber, her turban had unraveled. Waves of blond hair spilled over her shoulders—liquid gold shimmering in the sunlight.

Carelessly, she ran her fingers through the strands.

"You will protect me?" The timbre of his voice deepened, too, but his was not from sleep.

"You don't think I could?" Her eyes studied him, the blue darkening to indigo in challenge. So dark, he wondered how deep the irises turned with passion.

"Well?" she prompted. Annoyed, she swept the thick tresses to her back and sat up.

"I—"

Quamar jerked his head toward the east, his back stiff, his stance predatory.

"What is it?"

Deliberately, he placed his finger against his lips.

He waited for the flash of understanding to cross Anna's features, then handed Rashid to her open arms.

"Stay," he whispered tonelessly. When she started to turn away, he snagged his pistol from its holster and handed it to her. "Use this if necessary."

When she started to protest, he frowned. "Stay," he ordered again, then grabbed his rifle from the boulder nearby.

Born to the desert, he moved easily over the sand, his eyes alert, his body tight with caution.

The sun beat down, its glare like a thousand razors slicing through Quamar's scalp, reminding him too late that he still hadn't taken his pills.

"It is Farad! Do not shoot, Master Quamar."

Quamar swung around, almost lost his footing. Dizziness assailed his senses. Still, he held the rifle level.

A little man trudged over the ridge, his hands in the air. Leather reins ran from his fingers to a camel plodding lazily behind.

"I have brought good news and a gift—"

"Stay there!"

Farad stopped a hundred feet away and dropped to the ground. Quamar took his time walking to the man, examining the terrain as well as the surrounding area.

"Look at me, not the ground." When Farad didn't react fast enough, Quamar lifted him up by the back of his shirt. Quamar's arm trembled, and he tightened his hold. "How did you know where to find us?"

"You made it very difficult. Only by Allah's guiding hand could I have found you so quickly." Farad smiled, displaying gaps between his teeth.

Quamar tucked the rifle under Farad's chin, deliberately pushing it so the little man had to strain to keep eye contact. "I should kill you now, thief. And rid the world of one more pestilence."

This time it was Farad who shook, his small body convulsed with the tremors. "Please, Master. I will explain my presence if you release me."

"You are under the assumption I am interested in your explanations, Rat." He dropped Farad and grabbed the camel's harness. "I am only interested in your absence."

"Do you not want to know why I brought you this camel? One that gives milk. Or why I helped you in Taer?"

"You saw us in Taer, so you would know we had the baby," Quamar responded, his voice raspy as he fought the nausea that rolled in his belly. "As to why you followed us, you must have a death wish."

Quamar's head throbbed, the waves of dizziness increased. "Go home." When Farad started to protest, Quamar turned and pointed the rifle at his forehead. "Or die here."

"Quamar, please," cautioned a soft voice.

"Why are you not at the lean-to?" Quamar scowled. "This is not a tea party, Anna."

Farad caught the hint of compassion in Anna's voice and dropped on his knees at her feet. "I mean you no harm. Nor do I wish to hurt Prince Rashid," he added hastily.

Quamar snorted, then grimaced when the sound reverberated through his head. But his eyes never left Farad. "Do not get too close, Rat."

Anna shifted Rashid to her hip, instinctively putting herself between the baby and the thief. In her other hand, she gripped the pistol.

Quamar grunted his approval.

"Why do you call him Rat?" Anna asked.

"It is my name, Miss. Or at least, my—what do you call—nickname." He nodded his head with vigor. "Yes?"

"Yes," Anna responded slowly. "But why Rat?"

Quamar sighed, exasperated. "Are you looking at him, Anna?"

"I have a talent for escaping from small places," Farad explained.

"I see." Anna almost smiled at his enthusiastic

response, but the wind shifted and she caught a whiff of his scent. Instinctively, she took a step back.

The name Rat seemed appropriate in more ways than one. The little man smelled worse than a New York City dump. "Mr.—"

"Farad. Please call me Farad."

"All right. Farad," Anna agreed. "Why are you here?"

"His reasons are unimportant," Quamar responded. The briskness of his tone warned Anna not to ask any more questions.

She ignored it. "They're important to me."

Farad's gaze darted quickly from Anna to Quamar.

"I am afraid, Miss Cambridge. I was tolerated by King Jarek. But now, with the king imprisoned, I fear for my life." Farad shivered.

"You mean dead, don't you?" Quamar stepped toward the thief and prodded him with the rifle. "Jarek is dead."

"Dead?" Farad responded, frowning. "King Jarek is not dead."

Quamar grabbed Farad by the throat this time and brought the thief close until their faces were mere inches apart. "How do you know?"

"I… I saw him. And Queen Saree." Farad choked out the words while Quamar's grip tightened. He locked both hands on Quamar's wrists, but had little strength against the giant. "As of last night, they were both alive and being held by the Al Asheera in the palace."

"And if you were in the palace, just how did you escape?" Quamar demanded. Pain cleaved Quamar from skull to chin, forcing him to drop the little man.

"The sewer."

"The sewer—" He'd waited too long. When he straightened, his vision doubled. Quamar reached for his pills, but the earth tilted beneath his feet.

Anna cried out as Quamar crumpled to the ground.

"What did you do?" Anna pointed the pistol at Farad. "What did you do to him?"

"Nothing." Farad dropped to his knees and placed his hands together in prayer. "By Allah's hand, may I be struck down. I did nothing."

"Step back."

"But I can help." Farad grabbed for Quamar. "We must drag him out of the sun and into the shade."

When he jerked Quamar's arm, the pill container rolled out of the giant's hand.

"Back up, Mr. Farad."

"It's just Farad." When Anna quirked her eyebrow, Farad raised his hands in the air and took a few steps back.

"On the ground. Face down. Hands behind your back where I can see them." Anna reached Quamar and kneeled in the sand, her eyes never leaving the thief.

When Farad had done what she asked, she placed Rashid in the sand beside her. He immediately crawled on top of Quamar.

"Quamar," Anna said, using her hands to slap him awake. When he didn't respond, she grabbed the bottle then read the label.

"We must move him into the shade," Farad interjected. "The sun will make his illness worse."

Anna glanced at the lean-to, then pointed the gun once again at Farad. "No, you're going to move the shade to him."

Chapter Ten

Quamar fought the darkness, battling the steady thumping in his skull. His eyes blinked open, once, twice before he adjusted to the glare of the sun.

Quamar forced his eyes to focus.

The first thing he saw was Farad jabbing the first lean-to stick into the sand next to his head.

With a growl, Quamar reached out, grabbed the stick and tossed it to the ground. He jerked to his feet.

Anna stood a yard away, holding the baby in one hand, the pistol in the other. Relieved his stupidity hadn't cost them their lives, Quamar forced his muscles to relax.

He shook his head, testing the hammers, clearing the fog from his mind. The ache still throbbed at his temples, but the intensity was bearable.

Enough of the bitter, chemical taste remained

in his mouth to tell him that Anna had given him his pills.

"I guess I had to protect you sooner than either of us had anticipated."

Quamar scowled, but didn't answer.

"Why didn't you tell me *you* experienced fainting spells?"

"Because I do not faint," Quamar answered, each syllable short, clipped. Then instantly regretted the action when the hammers morphed into clubs. Without thinking, he rubbed the scar, trying to ease the tension beneath.

"Do most people carry prescription painkillers here because of the sun?"

"I get headaches. Migraines," he snapped, not liking to explain his illness.

"From what?" Anna's gaze studied him, but when he turned away, she saw his hand smooth the jagged white line at his temple. "Is it because of your wound?"

Quamar rubbed his hand over his face. "Yes."

When he didn't expound on his answer, Anna continued. "Will the pain go away?"

Quamar stopped, deliberately making his stance wider. "Yes, it will eventually go away," he lied. "The scar tissue interferes with the blood flow, causing the vessels to contract. When that happens, I get migraines."

"What can be done?"

"Nothing, Anna. But it is okay. I will be fine," he lied again. But this time, after seeing the worry in her eyes, the lie didn't sit well. "It is something I have learned to live with. Unfortunately, I did not take the medication soon enough. But I feel much better, I promise you."

He held out his hand for the pistol. She bit her lip, but didn't relinquish the weapon.

"What's the matter?"

"You cannot kill Farad, Quamar."

"I agree." Quamar stood, waiting, his hand still extended. After a moment, she placed the weapon in it. "I need him to guide me back into the palace."

Anna felt a rush of relief and covered her reaction by gathering up her robes. The thought of Quamar murdering didn't sit well. "We have plenty of water and food. It seems your Rat friend scavenged pretty well before he left the city. He packed extra provisions on the camel before he followed us."

"Anna," Quamar murmured, then tilted her chin up until her eyes met his. "Even if Farad had not told me about the palace, I would not have killed him."

When she nodded, he let go. "I might have hurt him a little, though."

He ignored her gasp and took the pill bottle out of his pocket. With a vicious twist, he opened the bottle, then placed two tablets beneath his tongue.

"How many of those can you take?"

"As many as I need."

Quamar walked over to Farad, who hovered by the camel. "You are safe for now, Rat. Simply because I will need you later to get inside the palace."

"Back inside?" Farad repeated. "But it was only by Allah's grace that I escaped the first time, Master. Surely, you don't—"

"Oh, yes I do," Quamar answered, his knife appearing in his hand. "Either help me later, or die now. Choose."

Farad looked at the blade. "I will show you."

"Good," Quamar said. "Right now, you can see to the camel. The baby will need milk soon."

"Yes."

"And, Farad, you will be drinking the milk first, so make sure it is not tainted."

When Quamar swung around, he noticed Rashid make a grab for Anna's hair. "You need to put your turban back on, Anna."

Rashid fisted the hair and tugged. Anna yelped, then laughingly pulled the few strands free. "Scamp," she whispered, and kissed the baby's forehead. "If you keep that up, I'll be as bald as your uncle."

"Let us hope not," Quamar responded, his gaze sliding over the strands blowing in the breeze. He fought the urge to move closer, to catch the hair himself, breathe in its fragrance.

"After Farad brings you the milk, you can feed Rashid. We start walking again late afternoon and will not stop until after dusk. Tomorrow, we start at daybreak and stop again at noon for rest. We will repeat the schedule for the next two to three days."

"And what are you going to do?"

"I want to have a talk with our thief," Quamar commented dryly.

"A talk?" Farad squeaked. Although how he got any words past the erratic bobbing of his Adam's apple, Quamar couldn't be sure.

"Among other things." Quamar folded his arms and deliberately stepped forward until Farad's head threatened to snap backward.

Quamar needed to gain some ground in case the thief took his brief faint for a sign of weakness. "First we are going to talk. Then I am going to search your belongings." He looked pointedly at the camel's supply packs. "After that, I am going to search you. I do not like surprises. If I come across one, you will not like it either. That is a guarantee."

"But, Master—"

"Make no mistake." Quamar spoke with even

tones. "The only reason you still live is because I am willing to believe, for now, that you know the sewer tunnels beneath the palace. But if you betray us, even that will not save you."

Anna shivered at the promise in Quamar's voice, but she certainly didn't argue. After all, Quamar had told her he wouldn't kill the thief. Right?

Right, the little voice whispered from the back of her mind.

"IT'S BEAUTIFUL, ISN'T IT?" The evening wind came in long, cool bursts over the sand dunes, now washed in pink and gold hues from the fading sun. "I always thought the desert was nothing but an endless sea of sand and dunes."

"A good part of it is," Quamar said, then adjusted his view to keep Farad in his sights. "The Sahara covers over three million square miles of terrain. We have yet to reach the most dangerous."

"It's so dry, so hot. I have a hard time imagining that anything survives out here." Anna's fingers automatically brushed over Rashid's bangs while the baby slept snugly in his sling.

"Many animals do. Some feed on the bugs, the sporadic plants. Others feed on each other."

They had just started their evening trek. Both Anna and Quamar had forgone their scarves and sunglasses in the dusk of the evening, enjoying the cooler breeze that came with it.

"Is that safe, letting him ahead of us like that?"

Farad trudged over the next ridge of sand with the camel in tow. A moment later, he all but disappeared on the other side.

Quamar's eyebrows raised in surprise. "I can still see him," Quamar responded, his tone just short of insulted. "He is not a threat, Anna."

Anna grinned, unable to stop herself.

"You think questioning my competence is funny?"

"No, but your reaction is." When he scowled, she laughed outright. "I was merely curious, Quamar. I know you are more than capable of taking care of us."

He nodded, but his scowl remained.

"How long have you been a soldier?"

His gaze returned to the horizon and Farad. "Since I was too young to know better."

When he didn't elaborate, Anna frowned. Maybe it was better not knowing about him. Although not sure why, Anna found herself drawn to him.

Maybe it was his strength. Certainly it wasn't his arrogance.

"And before?" she prodded, unable to stop herself.

"At one time my interests included only birds

and sports," Quamar offered. "And then later, women."

Startled, she stared at him, completely forgetting about her decision moments before. "Birds? As in ornithology?"

"I did not get the chance to truly study them." Quamar's mouth lifted slightly into a smile. "But I enjoy watching them." He paused for effect. "And the birds, too."

Anna laughed.

Suddenly, Rashid squirmed and let out a small, irritated cry.

"Okay, handsome. I didn't mean to wake you."

"Let me." Quamar took the baby and placed him into the crook of his arm. Once they started walking again, Quamar bounced Rashid up and down.

The baby screeched with delight.

"Does he need a change?"

Quamar patted the baby's bottom and shook his head. "We can travel a little longer."

"I think I could live here," Anna mused. "There's something about the land that tugs at you, isn't there?"

"Yes," Quamar murmured. "Every so often when I was younger, I would hear the wind whistling in the distance and watch the sands swirl and ebb, tempting me on a new adventure."

"Did you go?"

"Oh, yes. And many times paid for my foolishness." Quamar raised Rashid over his head. When the baby tried to grab at his turban, he brought him back down, laughing. "Never underestimate the Sahara. She enjoys punishing those who disrespect her authority."

"She?"

"My mother would say that the Sahara was a beautiful but wildly jealous woman who captured men's hearts and never let them go."

"Because of you and your father?"

"Yes, and her father, too," Quamar added. "That was how my parents met. My grandfather was a famous Italian photographer. Salvador Bazan. He specialized in photographing the deserts of the world. My mother, Theresa, accompanied him on one of his trips and she met my father. Soon after, or maybe instantly, they fell in love. Being royalty, my father could not leave the desert, so she stayed." Quamar shrugged. "And died here."

"Theresa Bazan was your mother?"

"Yes. You have heard of her?"

There was pride in his voice, enough to make Anna's lips twist into a smile. "Who hasn't? Your mother won a Pulitzer for her pictures on the desert people, the nomad tribes. Right?"

"Yes."

Then Anna remembered. "She died shortly after, didn't she?"

"Less than a year later." Quamar stopped, but his eyes remained on the horizon. "She died in my arms after being gutted by an Al Asheeran soldier. I was thirteen."

Anna thought of the boy who became a man that day. Tragedy had a way forcing people to grow up instantly. "Quamar," Anna said. Her hand found his arm and squeezed, stopping them both in the sand. "I am truly sorry."

The honesty behind her words made him look at her. But it was the sheen of unshed tears in her eyes that forced him a step closer. Deliberately, he shifted Rashid to his hip. "Do not underestimate the Sahara, Anna. Women are far more dangerous than most men. And she is no different."

"You believe that?" Her words this time were little more than a whisper. "That I'm—"

"Dangerous?" Quamar murmured, his hand cupping her chin, his thumb brushing over her bottom lip. "Yes, I do." With hooded eyes, he slowly leaned into her, giving her plenty of time to pull away.

But Anna couldn't. Her breath caught on his scent. Dry, wild, exotic.

Leisurely, he nibbled her top lip. She caught a taste of him. Hot. Foreign. Excitement fluttered through her throat. Aware of the baby between them, she shifted onto her toes, stretching.

His hand slid from her chin to her cheek, cupping the side of her face, framing her features. It was her only warning.

Suddenly, his mouth slanted over hers, diving, savoring. Desire punched her, knocking her off balance. When her knees buckled, she locked a hand around his wrist, holding herself up, holding him in place.

One of them groaned. Who, she wasn't sure. Didn't care because the sound triggered Quamar to go deeper, ravishing her mouth, filling her senses until she thought of nothing but him, tasted nothing but him.

Yearned for no one, but him.

"Master Quamar! It's coming!"

Quamar jerked away with such force, Anna stumbled back. Quick reflexes had him catching her elbow, steadying her and muttering a curse about tiny men.

Anna drew in a shattered breath, trying desperately to gain some control of the passion that raged within.

The wind shifted, grew stronger until bits of sand and grit whipped around them, stinging any exposed skin. Quickly, Anna grabbed Rashid, placed him under her robes for protection.

"Master Quamar! It's coming. The sand, it's coming!" Farad ran, his hand clamped down on the camel's harness, his feet tripping more than once as he raced down the hill.

"What is he talking about, Quamar?"

Then Anna saw. Like a monster it rose over a hundred feet in the air. Its fangs bared as it bore down on Farad with enough force that blasts of sand and grit would take skin off any man. Living or dead.

"A shzma!" Quamar bit down on a curse. But this time, Anna echoed the words.

Chapter Eleven

Quickly, Quamar grabbed the camel's headgear from Farad. "Get the blankets!" With deft fingers, the little man untied the bundle from the camel's saddle.

Quamar tugged the camel down until it lay in the sand.

After hobbling the animal, Quamar grabbed Anna to his side, placing the camel between them and the storm. "Burrow next to the camel, keep Rashid between you and the animal."

Anna had shifted Rashid in front of her just as Farad reached them. The little man grabbed two of the blankets and tossed one to Quamar.

Rashid screamed as Anna tucked him against her belly and huddled next to the camel's back. Already Farad was curled against the camel's hips.

Quamar quickly settled behind them, shielding

them with his body before covering all three of them with the blanket.

"The camel?" Anna whispered.

"She will be fine." Quamar tucked his arm under Anna's head, braced his other over both her and the baby. "Camels are born to the desert."

Within seconds, sand and dust clogged the air. Howling, it battered them. Anna didn't move, keeping Rashid in the small pocket between her and the camel.

"Don't let him die, Anna," the voice whispered. Anna concentrated on the baby's cries, welcoming them. If he cried, he could breathe.

Save him, Anna. He'll die.

No, he won't, she fought back silently.

The pitch of the wind heightened until it screamed around them. Anna's body shook, not from fear of the storm but from another fear. One that ran deeper, one that the voice fed on.

"It's all right, *Habbibi.* Shh. We are safe." Quamar gathered her closer, spooning her body into his while his hand held the blanket firmly over the three of them. Rashid's cries turned to whimpers and soon the little boy seemed quieted. The wind soothed him, or maybe it was Quamar's hushed murmurs.

Anna concentrated on Quamar's voice, lulled by the soft timbre. He talked to her in both Italian and Arabic. Words she didn't understand, but it didn't matter. The thick part of his arm rested under her head. Giving in to temptation, she kissed the skin beneath his lips, heard his breath hiss by her ear. Then felt the warm touch of his mouth against her temple.

Calmed now, between the man's heartbeat behind her and the baby curled against her chest, Anna relaxed.

Suddenly, as quickly as the storm began, it ceased.

Quamar threw off the blanket, covered beneath inches of sand. Anna scooped up Rashid, who had quieted somewhat, except for the occasional hiccup.

Farad stood, his dark skin spotted white.

"You did tell me your lady Sahara was the jealous type," Anna mused. "I just never guessed how jealous."

Quamar frowned, then remembered they had been kissing when the storm started. "We need to continue. If anyone is behind us, they will get hit with the storm. We have to make up time."

Anna stiffened, confused by the hard edge to his order. "What's the matter?"

"Nothing," Quamar snapped. "Nothing important, anyway."

Anna ignored the hurt beneath her heart and

concentrated on Rashid. “I need to change the baby before we go.”

Anna soothed Rashid, letting him play with her scarf while she walked over to the camel. “Good girl, Morgiana.”

“You named the camel?” Quamar asked.

“It just came to me.” Anna shrugged, still hurt from his order. “Morgiana was a character in—”

“*Ali Baba and the Forty Thieves.* The slave girl.”

“Yes,” Anna said noncommittally. “It was a favorite of mine growing up. Rather than deal with all the attention my father brought to my life, I buried myself in books.”

The urge to ask her more questions tugged viciously at Quamar. He wanted to ask if her childhood had been lonely. If she had any special friends. Anyone who shared her secrets.

In his mind’s eye, he could see the little girl curled in a chair, hidden from prying eyes while she read. Then later, the woman doing the same.

Questions brought people closer, and he couldn’t take the risk. He’d already allowed her further into his heart than he should have. If he allowed her any further, it would cause only pain for both of them.

He had told her the truth when the rebels had attacked Taer. He had come home to the desert. To his family.

But what he hadn't told her…

He had also come home to die.

THE SUN WAS GONE and still the heat pressed in on Anna. Sweat trickled down her back under her binding, stinging at the point between her shoulder blades.

"Princess Anna, may I help you with the camel?"

Using the back of her hand, she wiped the sweat from her forehead. "Please call me Anna, Farad."

"Are you not the daughter of the United States president?"

"Yes, but—"

"Then you would be considered a princess here."

Anna sighed. She just didn't have the energy to argue right now. Since the moment Rashid had woken up earlier, he had been difficult. Nothing she did made him happy. For an hour he alternated between temper tantrums and whimpers, each interrupted only when he chewed on his fist.

At one point, Farad had suggested the baby might be teething and gave Rashid a piece of leather to chew on.

The baby quieted immediately, happily chewing and drooling over his new teething toy.

At that moment, Anna softened to the little man.

"Can I help you, Princess?"

Anna held up the plastic bottle in her hand.

"Rashid dumped his milk into the sand. My fault I'm afraid for not realizing the cap wasn't on the bottle tight. I'm trying to get Morgiana to give me more milk while Quamar watches Rashid."

"If you hold the bottle, I will help Morgiana to fill it for you."

Anna nodded and scooted over to give Farad room. Morgiana turned briefly and looked at Anna with what appeared to be disdain.

"Is there anything you don't know, Farad?" Anna asked.

"I am sure there is much." He took the camel's teats gently between his fingers. When he pulled, milk filled the bottle.

"You know about camels, and teething babies."

Farad shrugged. "I am one of many children. You watch. You learn."

"So how did you become a thief?"

He hesitated, ready to play on Anna's compassion. "We were poor and I was small. Sickly. One night my father decided he had one too many mouths to feed. I was left behind," he said, surprised the hurt was still there, deep in his gut. He hadn't talked about his childhood in years. Had no one really to share his thoughts with.

"And your mother allowed it?" Anna whispered, the shock almost palpable.

"Yes."

"And your brothers and sisters?"

"I do not know, Princess. It was another time. Another country. Another life." He remembered the sharp pangs of an empty belly, the cold that had seeped into the bones and stayed for days on end. He had learned very early to protect himself from both—and from the predators. "That's one of the reasons I live in Taer. They tolerate the poor with much more kindness than most countries," Farad added, then stopped, suddenly realizing something. "That will change now with Hassan ruling. There is no fairness in Master Quamar's uncle. No humanity."

Anna's hand slipped over Farad's shoulder and squeezed. "Not if we have anything to do about it? Right?"

He glanced up at her, saw the sincerity and for the first time in his life wanted to believe.

Mentally he shook himself. He was here for one reason. Money. Wealthy people bought comfort, bought security. Quickly, he finished filling the bottle.

"Thank you, Farad." Slowly, Anna stood. When she paused, he looked up. "If I had been your family," she murmured, "I never would have left you behind."

Farad forced his lips to curve in a grateful

smile. In less than a day, he had succeeded in gaining Anna Cambridge as an ally.

But while his gaze followed her across the camp, his chest tightened. Not in elation or even satisfaction.

But with shame.

"THAT WAS QUITE A conversation you were having with the thief," Quamar commented as Anna took Rashid from his arms.

Anna chuckled when baby grabbed for the bottle. "This time, young man, no playing."

Rashid didn't spare her a glance, and instead raised the bottle to his mouth and started drinking the milk with short, greedy swallows.

"I like Farad, Quamar." Anna brushed Rashid's bangs off his forehead with gentle fingers. "Which is more than I can say for you right now."

"Oh, you like me, Anna Cambridge. The trouble is you like me too much." For a moment Anna thought Quamar was jesting, but there was nothing but hardness in his tone. "And I am having a hard time not reciprocating."

"I didn't realize 'too much' applied to any kind of friendship," she said, duplicating the hardness with her own words.

"We are not talking about friendship."

Her head jerked up. "If you're worried about

me falling in love with you, don't," she answered flippantly.

"Not love," Quamar admitted.

Her back stiffened, her chin hitched.

"But there is something."

"An attraction?" Anna asked, unable to keep the tremble out of her voice. "Lust? Is that what you're saying?"

"What I am saying is…" The bite was back in his words. "Whatever this—" his finger pointed back and forth between them "—is, dies now. Dies here."

"Fine," Anna snapped. "Anything else?"

"Sleep. We can get some sleep."

"Together?"

"Yes, together. We'll need the body heat to keep us and the baby warm." The only solace she had was that he sounded like a man struggling for his last breath.

"On the ground." It was a statement, not a question.

"Yes, on the ground." Quamar's eyes narrowed. *"Anything else?"*

Anna's brow raised when she saw his muscle jaw flex. Giving in to her impulse, she smiled sweetly. "Just one thing," she purred.

"What?" he growled, impatient.

"Do you prefer top or bottom?"

A CHILL FILTERED through the midnight air. Farad, no stranger to the cold, curled up against Morgiana, waiting. Three hours had passed since the camp settled. Quamar slept, one arm around both child and woman, his rifle near the other.

His fate lay in the timing. If the baby woke before his return, he failed. Patience, this time, meant survival.

Farad crept over the sand, cognizant of disturbing sleeping scorpions or poisonous vipers. Zahid had given him specific instructions. Head north until his men appeared. They were close enough to monitor, but far enough away not to be discovered.

Almost a half hour later, a sword jabbed the back of his neck. His hands went into the air. "We did not think you would show, thief."

There were four of them, their expressions cloaked behind their Al Asheera scarves. But Farad understood, with these men loyalty was given to the highest bidder. Men traded scarves as fast as coins changed hands.

Farad stood his ground as the men closed in, each bigger than the last. The tallest only a half a head shorter than Quamar himself.

The steel tip of a sword moved until it prodded Farad's Adam's apple. "I have made a bargain with Zahid," Farad said.

"And your word means so much, Rat," the one with the sword observed.

"Yes," Farad answered, assuming the man with the sword was their leader. "When profit is involved."

The sword lowered. "So, where is Sheik Bari's encampment?"

"I don't know," Farad replied, letting his arms fall to his sides. "I cannot get the information from his son. I do know that we are heading there but how many days or if we change directions, he won't say."

The leader took a step toward Farad, forcing the little man to back up. Farad bumped the man behind him and was shoved forward again.

"He's not making a straight line, that's for sure," another complained.

"Nor is he stopping for water," a third man, the smallest of the foursome, added.

"We'll need water tomorrow," Farad commented. "I've been spilling extra to deplete our supply whenever we rest. We are to leave at daybreak. Stop at noon. Continue on a few hours before dusk."

"Come see us tomorrow night, little man," the leader warned. "And use your time wisely. Zahid would be much happier if you knew where this encampment was before you actually reached it."

"I will do my best," Farad answered. He salaamed and hurried away.

"It's the woman and child that Zahid wants. Quamar is worth nothing once he reveals the camp's position," their leader commented. "I wonder how much Zahid is paying the thief."

The four men watched the darkness swallow Farad.

"Whatever the payment, it's more money than we are getting I'm sure," said the smallest. "Why do we need a middle man? If Zahid wants answers along with the woman and child…" A knife appeared in his hand. "I know how to get answers."

After a long pause, the leader's lips curved into a wide, vicious grin. "Maybe we should plan our own surprise."

Chapter Twelve

When Farad neared the camp, he could hear Morgiana snoring. Relief tripped through him. If he'd been discovered, the animal would've woken up.

Still, he could not get the image of the four Al Asheera out of his mind. A bargain had been made, but harming his princess or the baby hadn't been part of the deal.

His princess? When had he started thinking of her as his princess?

"Have a good trip, Rat?"

Farad jumped and would've screamed, except Quamar covered his mouth, and his fingers dug into the little man's jaw. "You wake up the baby, and you will suffer."

Farad nodded and waited. When Quamar let go, he tested the soreness in his jaw.

"Where were you?" The moonlight shone

across the giant's face, his black eyes glowed in the darkness.

"I thought I heard something, Master."

"What?"

For an instant, Farad thought about turning in the four men but immediately decided against the idea. He would risk uncovering his own deception. "I-I don't know. I could not find anything."

"Yet you were gone quite a while."

"Once I determined we were safe, I found a place to relieve my bladder." Farad waited. When Quamar didn't respond, he continued. "In the darkness." Again, he waited. "For some privacy," he finally added.

"So, you are telling me you are not hiding anything? No secrets? Or maybe…friends?"

Farad, sure that the giant was guessing, kept his expression bland.

"But then, we know you do not have any friends. Right?"

"None," Farad agreed. "But I do have many enemies." The words came out before Farad could stop them. But the truth jabbed at him. On its heels came his pride. So what, he had chosen his path, had he not?

"Oh, do not worry about them, Rat," Quamar admonished, pulling a rope from his belt. "Worry about me."

QUAMAR AWOKE AN HOUR before dawn, taking care not to disturb Anna and Rashid. During the night, both had curled into his side for warmth.

The dark smudges beneath Anna's eyes told him she hadn't slept well.

Quamar watched for a few minutes longer, unable to take his gaze off the woman and baby in her arms. A yearning grew deep in his belly. He had no problem picturing Anna with a child of her own. His child, he admitted.

Farad had long before gone to sleep by Morgiana, his hands tied to her hobble rope. The little man had proven himself useful over the past day, but still Quamar wasn't going to trust him. Once a thief, always a thief.

He heard it then. A clink of steel. As if someone was unsheathing a sword. Quickly, he shook Anna's shoulder until her eyes blinked, then grabbed his own sword. "Something or someone is out there, in the darkness. Stay behind me with the baby."

His blade barely cleared leather when he heard the battle cry across the sands. There were four. All Al Asheera. All charging with raised swords in the semidarkness.

He swung his blade toward the first soldier, sliced him in the leg, heard his scream just as another charged.

"Quamar!" Anna yelled. "Behind you."

Quamar glanced back, caught the man with his shoulder and flipped him into another.

"Get down!" Quamar bellowed, when a third Al Asheera stepped into the fray.

Anna hit her knees in the sand, felt the swoosh about her head. "Save Rashid!" Quamar came up, steel clashed steel. He kicked another in the stomach, sending him tumbling into the sand. "Go, Anna! Over the dune. Stay low in the shadows of the sand. I will find you!"

Quamar turned his attention back to the four men. They had chosen swords and knifes. Quamar saw no guns. Probably didn't want to risk shooting the woman and baby.

So be it, he thought grimly. He wanted nothing more than to work off some of his frustration.

With a sword in one hand, he waved them forward. He taunted them, calling Hassan's men whores in Arabic, satisfied when anger turned their stances rigid.

"Remember, we want him alive," the nearest Al Asheera yelled.

"And I want you dead." Quamar circled back, drawing their eyes toward him, placing his back to where Anna lay hidden.

"Where is the thief?" one asked, as his eyes flickered through the darkness.

A knife caught the man in the throat. His words

died as the blood choked and bubbled. "Here I am," Farad said, his voice menacing. He rolled shoulder-first into the sand, grabbed the dead man's sword and came up on his feet, successfully putting the remaining three men between him and Quamar. "Do you need any more of my help, Master Quamar?"

"Leave them to me, Rat. Go find Anna. Protect her."

"Yes, Master." Farad hesitated for a moment, then followed Quamar's order.

"Come on, then," Quamar taunted, wanting it done. Needing to get to Anna and the baby.

The three men rushed him, their swords raised. Metal clashed. When the first lost his footing, Quamar caught his face with the back of his elbow and felt bone give. The man cried out with the pain and fell to his knees. Quamar twisted, throwing the other two off balance and buried his sword in the stomach of the downed man.

Anna's scream split the air. Quamar growled, fear clutched at his gut. He feinted left, shoved his blade into the next man, then grabbed the man's sword. When the other attacked Quamar's back, he twisted, catching the last man in the chest with his partner's weapon. Both men collapsed in the sand, dead.

But Quamar didn't see. He was running toward the ridge.

ANNA RAN, DESPERATE to save Rashid. She scrambled down the slope of the ridge, hitting the flat bottom land with both feet.

Suddenly the sand gave way under her. She screamed, automatically tightening her arms around Rashid when she tumbled to her knees.

Moist sand soaked her clothes, but Anna ignored it and tried to stand. Immediately, sand caught at her legs, sucking her back down.

Fear stabbed at her. Quicksand?

Carefully, she lifted one foot. But when her body shifted, the sand rose to her hips.

With slow, deliberate movements, she maneuvered Rashid high on her chest. He smiled a toothless grin, then blew bubbles with the drool that spilled over to his chin.

She bit back a shout for help. If Quamar was still fighting, distracting him could mean his death.

"Princess," Farad yelled.

"Over here. Be careful—I've fallen in quicksand." Anna tried to stand perfectly still, but Rashid started to wiggle when he saw Farad. Quietly, she tried to hush him, but the baby grabbed her hair and squealed.

The sand crept upward, reaching her chest. She scooted the baby higher.

The little man skirted the rim of the quicksand. "Do not move, Princess."

Farad yanked his turban from his head and with shaking fingers unwrapped the long, cotton scarf. "I will throw one end to you and will pull you free."

Anna caught the material easily and immediately wound it around her wrist before grasping it within her fist. "Go."

Farad pulled, digging his heels into the sand, straining until his body shook with the effort. Still, Anna didn't move.

"It's not working, Farad," Anna said, panting with sheer terror. "We're too heavy. The quicksand is sucking us down. You need to find Quamar—"

"Anna!"

Relief pricked behind her eyes and with it a sheen of tears. "Here, Quamar. We're here in the quicksand. Be careful."

Quamar stopped, taking in the situation with a glance. A cold sweat broke over his skin. "Everything will be okay," he said, reassuring himself along with her. "You just need to make slow, easy movements."

After dropping his sword, he lay on the

ground and stretched out his arm. "Can you maneuver closer?"

When she tried, she found herself sinking inches more. "No. The baby…we weigh too much."

With only his shoulders clearing the edge, Quamar found he could go no farther without going under, too.

"Maybe if she throws him to you, Master Quamar?" Farad asked.

Anna shifted, trying to ease the baby above her head. "I don't have the leverage or strength to get him across."

"Anna." Quamar pulled off his robe. "The trick with quicksand is to float on top." He unbuttoned his shirt. "Most quicksand is more water than sand."

"I can't."

"I know, *Habbibi.* I am going to do the floating. What I want you to do is hand me Rashid as soon as I reach you."

Farad grabbed Quamar's arm. "Let me, Master. I am lighter."

Quamar paused, considering. "All right." He nodded briskly. "Take off your robes and shirt. Their weight will only pull you down."

Farad stripped down to his loincloth. Slowly, he lay down with his back on the sand. His slight body shook with the cold or fear. Quamar didn't know which.

"I will hold your ankles, Farad, so you will not drown. Grab the baby first, otherwise they will both drag you under."

Inch by inch, Farad maneuvered closer, keeping his arms extended out on either side to stay afloat. Moments stretched to minutes while he made his way across. But finally, he lay only a few feet away.

"Princess, hand me the baby," he rasped, his body straining to reach them.

But Anna couldn't. Her body started shaking. *Rashid wouldn't be safe. Rashid would die.*

"Anna. Give Farad the baby," Quamar ordered.

"No, Rashid will drown."

"Princess. Please," Farad coaxed.

Quamar could tell she wasn't listening to them. Panic etched her features, made her eyes dart back and forth.

But Farad could not float on the sand more than another minute. Fear rose through Quamar, tasting of bile and sand. "Anna, listen to me! Rashid is not Bobby."

"I couldn't save him." Anna shook her head. "Can't save him."

"Yes, you can. Give Rashid to Farad."

Tears rolled down her face unchecked. "I can't.

If I leave him…" Her whisper broke and she clutched Rashid close.

"Anna, look at me." When she did, Quamar saw the anguish, the shadows of fear. "Trust me."

Again, she shook her head. Terror rolled through her, wave after wave battered her logic. Anna clenched her jaw, fighting for control.

"Close your eyes and hold him out, *Habbibi,*" Quamar whispered. "Please. I will save him. I promise."

"You will save him." Anna squeezed her eyes shut, purposefully picturing Quamar holding the baby. The strength of his arms as they tightened around Rashid, holding him still, holding him safe. Shaking, Anna extended her arms, her fingers tight on Rashid.

"Now, Farad!"

The thief grabbed the baby and Quamar yanked. The baby's scream rent the air, his hands still gripping strands of Anna's hair.

Quamar's muscles bulged, his body strained, but within a few seconds Farad and the baby lay free of the sand.

"Thank you," Anna whispered, not sure if she was thanking God or Quamar.

Sweat poured down Farad's face. He wiped the sting of it from his eyes while Quamar sat the baby on the ground. Immediately Rashid scrunched his face, then screamed. But blessedly he didn't move.

With Rashid safe, reason returned with blunt clarity. The sand level rose to Anna's neck. For the first time in her life, she understood the term being swallowed alive. The instinct to claw her way free overwhelmed her, but she clamped it down. With infinite care, she brought her arms straight out each side, hoping to stall the rising level.

"Ready?" Quamar prompted.

The thief nodded and once again lay on his back. After taking a long, deep breath, he scooted headfirst out over the quicksand.

"Farad cannot see you, Anna. You will need to reach for him."

Anna didn't dare nod. The sand engulfed her chin now, forcing her head back, her eyes up. "I will."

Unable to see, she reached out blindly, her hands slick with sand and slime. She felt hair first, matted with sweat to the little man's forehead. Instantly, his hands clasped hers. When her right slipped, his hand closed like a vise over her wrist.

"Now!"

Quamar yanked Farad. Her wrist pulled, then popped. Searing heat raced through her forearm. Anna groaned but held tight.

Almost immediately, Farad went under the

sand in spite of Quamar's struggle to stop him. Farad and Anna's weight combined couldn't have been much over two hundred pounds, but the sand sucked them back.

Straining, Quamar planted his feet and heaved, digging his heels in with each step back. Finally, Farad was out and Anna's knees cleared the quicksand.

Farad doubled over. He coughed in short hacking spasms, his body rejecting the sand he'd swallowed.

Exhausted, Anna crawled to the baby, then collapsed a few feet away. Rashid crept to Quamar, hiccupping his displeasure.

Without warning, Anna doubled over. Thousands of tiny razors seemed to slice at her chest and stomach, as if flaying her skin to the bone. She rolled in the sand, trying to smother the pain, trying to catch her breath.

When she groaned, Quamar jerked around.

"Make it stop."

She groped at her clothes, trying to remove them, but her right hand wouldn't work. "Quamar! Get it off me." The pain turned to agony.

He handed the baby to Farad. "Take him to safety, but do not go to far—there might be more quicksand."

Quickly, Quamar snagged his knife from his

boot and cut through her shirt. Stripped down to her binding, Anna stood before him, her body shaking, mournful whimpers coming from her throat.

Quamar caught the bottom of the binding and sliced upward with his knife. Anna groaned, but he didn't stop. Only when it lay at his feet, and she stood naked from the waist up in front of him, did he pause.

He let out a long hiss.

Raw welts striped her chest and stomach, some deep enough that blood pooled. Bits of sand and grit had worked their way into the open sores, causing the fiery pain.

Quamar grabbed his robe from the ground, shook it out and then placed it over her shoulders. Only then did he notice her wrist, now swollen twice its normal size. "You are all right, *Habbibi,* I have you." When he picked her up with a strong but gentle grip, she whimpered but did not protest.

"Farad," Quamar called. When the thief appeared over the ridge, he continued. "Keep the baby. When we get to camp, we will put Anna on Morgiana and get the hell out of here."

"And the dead men?"

"Leave them for the vultures."

Chapter Thirteen

Anna rode Morgiana while Quamar and Farad took turns carrying Rashid.

They traveled for hours until dunes gave way to large stone pillars that rose from the sand. More than a half-dozen, each different heights, all layered in lines of burgundy stone.

Just beyond lay houses made of matching mortar, most in ruins with no more than one wall. The wind worked through the cracks and windows in a low-pitched, tuneless whistle, a poignant tribute to the past.

"It's beautiful."

"It has water," Quamar responded.

"Really?" Exhausted, Anna had begun believing no water existed in the never-ending rolls and curves of the land.

"Enough to clean your wounds and, if you'd like, to bathe in," he added.

"Yes," Anna agreed. During the ride, the pain in Anna's skin had eased, all but in the worst areas under her arms, at the sides of her breasts. Her muscles screamed in protest the moment Anna tried to stretch the stiffness out.

"We are stopping here?" Farad asked. "But this is Maltri. The water ceased pooling here years ago."

"Look again, thief."

As they approached the ruins, Quamar circled toward the back. An old stone trough lay next to one of the pillars, and just beyond it stood a well. Quamar snagged a stone from the ground and tossed it into the opening.

The *plunk* of the water brought a smile to Anna's face. "Oh, it's wonderful."

Farad grabbed Morgiana's reigns and with one whisper and a small tug, convinced the camel to kneel.

"I think she likes you, Farad," Anna observed, smiling.

A blush spread over the little man's cheeks. "She is but a beast, Princess."

"But I think if she could talk, we would both agree you are a good man," Anna added. Startled, Farad looked at her.

"What you did for Rashid and me…" Anna offered softly. "Thank you for saving us."

Embarrassed, Farad could only nod.

"Come, Princess," Quamar interrupted, raising his arms to Anna. "Time to join us on land."

He helped her dismount, his hands more than spanning her small waist, careful not to touch her injuries. His initial intention had been to let her go, but when her body trembled with fatigue, he swooped his arm under her legs.

"What are you doing?"

"Carrying you," he responded. "You are exhausted and I do not want you collapsing on me."

"I wasn't the one who fainted yesterday."

Ignoring her remark, he carried her across the sand to one of the camel troughs and set her next to a nearby boulder. "There are two water troughs and a well. We can let Morgiana drink from one and refill our supply. Once she's done drinking her fill, I'll clean it out for you and Rashid."

"And this one?" Farad asked, grimacing at the water. "We will use this one to replenish our canteens?"

"No." Quamar walked up behind Farad. "This one I have special plans for." He took Rashid, then nodded toward one of the stones. "Sit." Once she did, Quamar placed Rashid in the crook of her lap.

"I don't understand," Farad said, but he instinctively took three steps back as Quamar approached.

"I have had enough, Rat." Quamar reached over and grabbed Farad by his collar. He lifted the little man off his feet and strolled to the trough. "I have spent the last twenty-four hours walking downwind from you. Your stench makes my eyes tear and my headaches worse. If I am to keep an eye on you, I would rather do it without dealing with your smell."

"Princess," Farad squealed, his hands slapping at Quamar's. "Please help me."

Rashid clapped, enjoying the struggles of the little man.

"Sorry, Farad," she declared, but her tone indicated anything but sorrow. Instead, Anna smiled and placed her hands over the baby's and helped him clap more.

"We must keep moving," Farad screamed in desperation. "We are in serious danger if we stay."

"Not so much danger that I will continue abiding your stink," Quamar bellowed. "You travel with me, you will not smell like a septic pool of human waste."

With a flick of his wrist, Quamar tossed Farad into the camel trough. "Wash yourself and your clothes clean. Or drown yourself, I do not care. Either way I will not be forced to deal with your stench any longer."

Quamar reached into Anna's pack and grabbed

the bar that Sandra had placed in there. "Here's some soap," Quamar said and tossed the bar to Farad. "Use it."

"If you'd like, I'll wash your clothes with ours later, Farad," Anna suggested. "I need to wash the baby's diapers, too."

"You would do that for me, Princess?" Farad frowned, taking the bar and giving in to the impulse to sniff. The soap smelled of clean leather and spice. "You are kind when kindness is not necessary. I'm nothing more than a thief."

"You are much more than that. You just haven't figured it out yet," she teased. "Place your clothes by the well when you are through."

Farad knew that he should smirk. After all, a princess washing a thief's garments?

Oh yes, he should smirk with delight.

But the lump in his throat stopped him.

THE TROUGH—POSITIONED behind two of the stone pillars—allowed Anna more than enough privacy for a bath.

But Quamar was taking no chances. Farad had been right, information about water holes traveled fast, even in the Sahara. And although Quamar had discovered the replenished well just over a week before, many others had probably done the same.

With rifle in hand, Quamar leaned against the nearby pillar, his back to Anna. In the distance, Farad conversed with Morgiana while the animal grazed, content now that she had been rehydrated.

Rashid screamed, alerting Quamar. He stepped from the pillar ready, his stance wide, then he froze.

Anna sat in the trough with Rashid on her lap. Both of them laughed as Rashid splashed the water into his face. She picked up the naked baby and blew air on his tummy, sending him into another squeal of laughter.

Somewhere in the back of his mind, Quamar knew he should turn away, give them privacy. But something inside, an ache under his heart, kept him immobile.

The sun washed over woman and child, leaving its light to sparkle from the water drops, contrasting her alabaster skin against Rashid's richer coloring.

While the trough was big enough to hold both Anna and Rashid, the sides barely covered her stomach, leaving most of her nakedness exposed to Quamar's gaze.

Rashid fisted a damp golden curl against Anna's shoulder and pulled. She screamed with mock indignation. "You little devil," she scolded, her loving tone diffusing her words. Rashid brought his fist to his opened mouth, ready to take a bite. Laughing, Anna tugged the lock free and used the end to tickle the baby's nose. Taking care with her injured wrist, she hugged him close. "You are a charmer, aren't you?"

Rashid looked up, patted Anna's face then hooked his index finger into her mouth. "I got you now," she murmured and lifted the baby up on her head until he squealed with delight. Not realizing the position left her body turned toward Quamar.

A shaft of desire speared his gut. The curve of her breast, the pink nipple tightening in the soft breeze every time she lifted the baby. For the first time in his life he could picture a baby—his baby—suckling at its mother's breast. Anna's breast.

And the image almost brought him to his knees.

"Quamar," Anna whispered.

"Anna, I'm—" Quamar's gaze caught hers, saw the flash of desire.

"Please, don't be sorry," she pleaded. "I don't think I could stand it if—"

"You are beautiful." Quamar counted to ten, more to steady the heat in his blood than to give her time.

"As beautiful as the Sahara?"

"More."

"Thank you." Anna hugged Rashid against her. "Would you come get Rashid for me, so I can finish my bath?"

Quamar grabbed the robe from beside the tub and held it to the baby. Deliberately he kept his gaze on Rashid. "Anna. You have no reason to trust me after this. But we need to tend to your wounds."

"I trust you."

Quamar's hands shook when he reached for the baby. "After you wash, I need to check the sores on your back to make sure all the sand is free," he explained, hugging Rashid. "You cannot afford an infection."

"All right," she agreed easily.

Suspicious, Quamar studied her for a moment.

"Give me ten minutes to wash my hair and finish bathing. I'll be ready then."

QUAMAR HELD RASHID, smiling when the baby grabbed at his nose. Gently, he pulled the little fingers away.

Suddenly, Farad stood beside them both. "I will take the prince, Master Quamar."

Rashid caught sight of the little man and smiled. He raised his arms and gurgled. "It seems," Quamar drawled, "you have won over someone else, Rat."

"The feeling is mutual, I assure you," Farad replied adamantly, hugging the baby. "I would give my life for him."

"Well, let us hope it does not come to that." Quamar's eyes strayed to the horizon. The afternoon was passing swiftly, and soon they needed to be on their way.

CONFIDENT HE'D GAINED control again, he returned to Anna.

"Are you ready?" Quamar asked quietly, determined to finish the chore and leave.

"Yes." Anna drew her knees up to her chest and leaned forward. Although the water was milky from soap, Quamar had a clear view of her body. His eyes grazed over her skin, down her spine to the soft curve of her derriere.

He knelt at the end of the trough, behind her. Ignoring the tremble in his fingers, he slowly brushed the wet locks from her back.

"They hardly hurt now," she whispered, her voice dropping to a husky murmur.

One by one, he checked the sores. "You are lucky." He, too, spoke in quiet tones, not wanting to shatter the intimacy. "Most are superficial and very few still need attention." Those at the sides of her breasts were deep enough that sand still clung to the raw pink skin.

He ripped a piece of linen from the bottom of his shirt and dunked it in the water. "Let me know if I hurt you."

She nodded, but said nothing. With his first touch, goose bumps spread across her back.

His heart rate quickened.

"What does *Habbibi* mean?"

"Why?" Startled, he tried to rein in his desire.

"I'm curious. You addressed me a few times by the name. The first time at the warehouse, then in the sandstorm, and then again by the quicksand."

"It is an Arabic endearment for 'my heart,'" Quamar said evenly. Then to lessen its importance he added, "It is a casual name."

"Like 'sweetheart'?"

"Yes, it does not mean anything, really," he added. But when she stiffened, regret rifled through him.

"Do you still work for my father, Quamar?"

"No." Unable to stop himself, he let two of his fingers drift down to the soft curve of her hip.

"Are you saying you retired? You're no longer an agent?"

Quamar nodded, not trusting his voice, then realized she couldn't see him. He cleared his throat. "I retired a few months ago, after a mission landed me in quarantine."

"Quarantine? What quarantine?"

"A biochemical weapon that got away from our government and into the hands of some terrorists. Myself, and a few other operatives were exposed."

"Was Cain MacAlister one of the operatives?"

Surprised, Quamar stopped for a moment. "No."

"My father said Cain worked for a special branch of the government. Covert ops. That's why he was with my father at the time of my grandmother's death," Anna explained. When Quamar didn't respond right away, she frowned. "Don't worry, I've learned to keep secrets."

"I am not worried, *Habbibi,*" he murmured.

Anna shivered, but remained silent.

"Cain was the first to realize there would be an assassination attempt on your father's life." Quamar eased the cloth up over ribs to the tender side of her breast. Her mouth parted, her eyes fluttered closed.

He froze. "Did I hurt you?"

"No." She opened her eyes once more but didn't look at him. Instead, she rested her cheek on her knees. "So if you were an operative, where are all your gadgets?"

He laughed. The vibration felt foreign, it had been that long. "I prefer technique to technology."

She smiled against her knees. "You have never laughed in front of me before. It's nice. You should do it more often."

"I just might." He moved the cloth over to her left side, gave in to the urge to skim his fingers across her skin, feel its moist, silky texture.

"Did you have a code name?"

He dropped his hand into the water, rinsing the rag. Then twisted it dry. Then dunked it again. "Yes."

"What was it?"

"Kratos."

"The Greek god?"

"Actually he was a demigod." He raised the rag up by her shoulder and squeezed. Droplets of water trickled over her shoulder blade and followed the curve of her back.

"Meaning half human, half god," Anna said, understanding. "I'm a little rusty on my mythology. What was he known for?"

"Strength. He was Zeus's tool for dispensing justice," Quamar said, then felt compelled to tell the rest of the truth. "I have a…friend. You might know him. His name is Jordan Beck."

"Jordan?" Anna asked, surprised. "I've met him several times, actually. His family is rather prestigious in London, something about being twenty-eighth in line to the crown."

"I did not know that, but yes, it sounds like Jordan." Quamar nodded.

"By *friend,* you mean he's an operative, too."

"Yes," Quamar answered, knowing in essence he was trusting her with another secret.

"Kratos. I've heard that name—" Anna's eyes snapped to Quamar's. "Operation Kratos. Isn't that the name given to the London police's shoot-to-kill policy for terrorists?"

"Very astute." Quamar smiled, liking the fact that not much got past Anna. "For a long time I was considered a terrorist threat to England. So hence the name, Kratos."

"That's kind of ironic, isn't it?"

"Exactly. Jordan loves irony." Quamar paused. Right now, Jordan would say this whole situation was pretty ironic. "Anna, I am not who you think I am," Quamar murmured. "I have killed so many."

"These people, were any of them innocent?"

"No."

"Did you save innocents?"

"Not always, but that was usually the objective."

"And now, since your retirement?"

When he didn't answer, she glanced over her shoulder. "You've been wandering ever since."

"Until lately, yes."

"You know, I've asked you a question…several times," Anna commented, resting her chin on her knees. "Each time you sidestepped it, or ignored it altogether."

"I would guess, then, that it was not a question I wished to answer," Quamar mused, in spite of his tense muscles.

"And now?" Anna turned her whole body so she could see his face, using her hands to cover her breasts. If he was to avoid the question again, he would do so face-to-face. "Why were you here, Quamar? Why did you come back at this time? Did you know about Al Asheera's impending attack?"

"No." Quamar sighed and sat back. "I saw the attack from my camp outside the city. By the time I reached the palace, the rebels had already overrun it."

"So you came back home to do some camping?"

"No, Anna." He dropped the rag back into the water, then looked out beyond the walls. The Sahara wind whispered in his ear, goading him. After a moment, he faced her again. "I came home to die."

Chapter Fourteen

"To die?" A cold knot formed in her stomach.

"While I was under quarantine a few months ago, the doctors noted that my headaches were getting steadily worse. Since I was stuck, so to speak, they decided to run additional tests on my head injury."

"The scar tissue?" she remembered aloud.

"Yes. It is growing. Within a few months it will impede most of the blood flow to the right side of my brain."

Suddenly, her body temperature dropped, her blood turned ice-cold. She hugged her chest, forgetting her nudity with the chill. "You mean you'll stroke out?"

"Or die from a seizure."

"And there is nothing they can do to help you?"

"No. There is nothing," Quamar lied. He did not mention the possible operation because the risk of coming out lobotomized was high. An unacceptable alternative.

"So you came to the desert to die. By yourself?"

Her words were an accusation, not a confirmation. Still he answered, hoping for understanding. "Yes."

"But you said you had a few more months." Again came the accusation, but this time anger rode on its heels.

"An estimate," Quamar stated. "But it does not matter. A few months, a few weeks. I had done everything I wanted to do. It was time."

"I never knew there was a time to roll over and die."

The jab hit a nerve, one he didn't realize existed until that moment. "Your anger will not change the outcome. Neither will your insults."

Suddenly, the anger left her. He was right, of course. "I'm sorry," she admitted. "Everybody dies. That's reality. But the hard part isn't the actual dying, is it? The hard part is accepting that death is a part of life and can't be avoided."

Anna leaned in and with her good hand, touched his scar. She ran her fingers over the ridges. But her actions didn't stop her tears from gathering. "Does it hurt now?"

"The pills help." His hand caught her fingers,

gently stopping the caress that hurt more than the injury.

"Maybe I can help more," she whispered.

Quamar fought for control, even as Anna's words, her scent filled his senses, drawing him in. Just one last time, he thought. A dying man's last request.

With a groan, his fingers sank into her hair, buried themselves in the thick, damp tresses. He locked her head between his palms and plundered her mouth.

Anna gasped, but didn't back away from the assault. His hand slipped over her breast, his thumb circled the nipple in slow, easy strokes. His tongue worked its way into the far recess of her mouth, tasting, coaxing. Arousing.

His lips slid down her throat, over her collarbone while his tongue tasted, then soothed the red marks on her skin.

"So tender," Quamar whispered. The husky timbre of his voice vibrated against the side of her breast, sending jolts of electricity skittering across her skin. "Like rose petals, so easily damaged."

"No, not so easily." Pushing away all doubts, Anna raised herself on her knees to give him more access, whimpering when he took his time.

His hands, slick with water, caressed her back in long, easy strokes. The tempo soothed, heated.

He followed the bumps of her spine with light fingers. Anna arched into him, stretching and rubbing, restless to get closer.

Once at the base, he slid to her backside, clutched, then moved his fingertips over its crevice until she moaned with pleasure.

Impatient, Anna followed his lead. Her hands moved over his chest, feeling the hard muscles bunch beneath her touch. Desperately, her fingers parted his shirt, wanting to feel her skin against his. She slid the shirt over his shoulders, trailing her fingers down his arms until the shirt lay in a pool by the tub.

When her chest brushed once, twice up against his, Anna shuddered with pleasure. She nibbled the base of his neck, felt his pulse jump beneath her mouth, delighted in the masculine taste of him.

"Anna." Her name came out in a tortured plea. Every sinew in Quamar's body tightened against hers, fighting for control.

But she showed no pity. Instead, her fingers slipped down over his belly. She paused when the muscles quivered beneath her touch before sliding to the drawstring of his pants.

Quamar hissed through his back teeth but didn't stop her from loosening the knot until her fingers dipped beneath the waistband.

Instead, he gathered her close. Then, in one easy movement, he stood, keeping her pressed to the hard lines of his body. Automatically, her legs encircled his waist, her hands grabbing his massive shoulders for balance.

Unable to stop herself, she shifted until the apex of her thighs pressed against the hardness between his. With a groan, she squeezed closer.

"Fall back," Quamar rasped. The order came from pain, a desperate need for release. "Trust me."

Anna's eyes met his, losing herself in the swirl of emotions. She realized then that she did trust Quamar—trusted the innate strength of him.

With a sigh she fell back, letting his arms catch her at the small of her back. The position made her vulnerable and for the first time in her life, she relished the feeling.

Her breasts thrust upward and Quamar caught a sensitive nipple between his teeth. Anna whimpered with pleasure, helpless to do anything but feel the rough touch of his tongue against the hard point.

In the distance, the baby laughed. Anna jerked, then stilled. "Rashid."

Quamar pulled her back to him until their foreheads slanted together, their breath mingling in warm, heavy gasps of air.

Reality slammed into Quamar, shattering the hard wall protecting his heart. Suddenly, he wanted it all. The wife, the children. Growing old next to the woman he loved. Growing old with Anna. The pain continued through his chest and into his throat, choking him. A life with Anna would never be his. And nothing would change that fact.

"Quamar, I think I might be falling in love—"

"This is impossible," Quamar said at the same time.

She jerked back as if struck.

"Anna—"

"Don't. Don't make it worse." Tears pricked behind her eyes and she blinked them back. With her good hand, she pushed against his chest until he released her. "I can finish my bath now, by myself," she said dully. She grabbed her robe from beside the trough and covered herself.

"Trust me, Anna. It is better this way."

But even as he stepped away, she whispered, "Better for who?"

DARKNESS SWIRLED, coiling at her feet. The little boy laughed and tugged at her hand. *"Come, Anna, play with me."*

Anna smiled and followed him until a forest rose up before her. His laughter bounced off the pines, but where he'd been, there were only dark, haunting shadows.

"Bobby?" Fear quickened her step. From where it came she didn't know, but the fear was there, clawing at her insides. Then she heard his scream of terror.

Anna ran, now desperate to get to Bobby. Tripping over stones and tree roots, she ignored the branches that caught at her shirt, snagged her hair.

"You left me! Now I'm dead!"

"No." Anna jerked awake, but his words followed her back from her dreams. "Oh, God. He's dead."

"Anna, it is a dream. You had a bad dream." Quamar gathered her close.

"Rashid?"

"He is safe, here next to me."

She saw Rashid, then, his arms flung out, his face soft with sleep.

Her heart pounded against her ribs; sweat dampened her hair and shirt. Maybe it was the warmth of his skin, or the sympathy in his voice, but something inside Anna crumbled. "No. It was a nightmare. One I thought I'd exorcised long ago."

Quamar gathered her close, rocked her back and forth. "About your brother?"

She jerked back. "How did you—"

"You said his name right before you woke up."

She nodded, allowing Quamar to pull her close once again.

"Do you get them often? The nightmares?"

"Every night for years after Bobby's death. Then less and less as time passed."

Quamar remained silent. Life could not be sidestepped or overlooked. The pain must be bared while the fortune must be rejoiced.

"Thank you."

Startled, Quamar looked at her. "For what?"

"For not saying I need to get over his death or some other trite phrase that people say."

Quamar nodded, understanding. "Tell me about him."

"You mean, tell you about his death."

"If that is the best way for you to describe him. Most people will show their true selves within the moments before they die. If they are cowards, their last words will be entreaty. If they have faith, their last thought will be of Allah."

"And if they are evil?"

"They will die with a curse on their lips and blood on their hands."

"Bobby died like he lived. Quietly." Anna leaned back, curving into Quamar's chest. "He was such a boy, though. Big eyes. Gangly, with pointed shoulders and elbows and huge feet. His feet were so big, he spent more time tripping over them than walking on them." Anna chuckled at the memory. It felt good for once. "He had a habit of running his hand through his hair. Happy, sad. Frustrated. Angry. It didn't matter. His hand was always jammed in his hair. The last time I saw him, it stood on end. It was lighter than mine." Her fingers fluttered over Rashid's hair. "Almost as white as Rashid's is black."

Anna felt Quamar's nod against her temple. The gentle movement prodded her to continue.

"It lay in soft spikes against his cheeks the day I left. He'd been crying, you see, because I'd decided to spend some vacation time with my friends. Bobby didn't want me to leave. He was so shy, he had a hard time making friends. Add the fact he was the president's son…Well…" She rubbed the shivers from her arms.

"You were young also."

"But I thought I was an adult. And I didn't want to spend my summer hanging out with my little brother. So I justified my decision by telling him he needed to grow up and get over his shyness. And stop depending on me." Her eyes met Quamar's and saw sympathy rather than pity. "When I left, Bobby hugged me and told me he loved me. Then he asked me one more time to stay. I said no." Memories slithered through her, their edges slick with guilt. "It was the last time I saw him alive."

"The nightmares?"

"After the funeral, I started having them," she explained. "Horrid dreams with me waking up beside him in his coffin, or playing with him in the forest. Hide-and-seek. It used to be his favorite game. In my dreams, I found him rotting in a tree trunk or under some vines."

Quamar brushed the hair from her forehead. "And tonight?"

"The same," Anna answered. "I thought I'd dealt with it. I guess protecting Rashid has brought it all back to the surface."

"Bobby was killed by the same man who killed your grandmother, wasn't he?"

Anna nodded. "And the same man who shot you, right?"

"Yes."

She waited, her lips twisting bitterly. "What? No comment about how I couldn't have prevented Bobby's death?"

"You forget I did not prevent your grandmother's death," Quamar said. "Both were targeted by an assassin who wanted to cripple your father's political career. It was my job to protect your grandmother."

"But that wasn't your fault—" Anna stopped.

"What our minds know to be true and what our hearts accept as the truth are not always the same."

"Quamar, my family never blamed you for my grandmother's death. You took a bullet while you were trying to protect her."

His chin rested on top of her head, but he said nothing. He wanted to ask her why she had come to see him in the hospital right after the shooting, but then disregarded the notion because it served no purpose. If she did it out of duty or kindness or some other reason, it wouldn't change his future, only make it harder to deal with.

"What are you thinking?"

"That we must get some sleep." Quamar tightened his hold to take the cruelty from his words.

For once, Anna didn't argue.

Soon, her breathing evened into sleep, and her silent tears dried against his skin.

But somehow he couldn't find the strength to loosen his arms.

RASHID'S LAUGHTER FILLED the air, bringing Anna fully awake. Automatically, she reached down for the baby, only to find him gone.

Anna bolted up, then relaxed immediately. He sat a few feet away, flinging small handfuls of sand and talking in a language only babies understood.

"Okay, handsome," Anna muttered, scooting behind Rashid. "Next time, wake me—"

Anna froze. A sand viper, no more than three feet in length, lay curled a short distance from the baby.

Rashid squealed and threw another handful of sand, coming dangerously close to the reptile. Fear rushed at her. With its head raised, its dark eyes fastened on Rashid, Anna knew the snake had reached its limit of patience.

Anna searched blindly behind her until her fingers touched the lean-to stick. With deliberate movements, she grabbed the stick and slowly pulled it, along with the robe, from the ground.

She extended her arms over the baby. If she acted too quickly, the snake might strike. The stick, already heavy from the robe's added weight, turned slippery in her sweat-slick hands.

Suddenly, Rashid saw her and let out another squeal. Anna threw the robe over the snake and yanked Rashid to her.

Rashid's squeals turned to screams.

Farad and Quamar running.

Anna cuddled the baby, soothing him. When the men reached her, she said, "There's a snake under the robe."

"Take the baby farther away, Anna." Quamar took the scene in with one glance. After unsheathing his sword, he used the tip to remove the robe.

"Master," Farad interrupted. "I will catch him.

I would like to milk him and use the venom for my knife."

Quamar studied him for a moment. "Get rid of it when you are done," Quamar ordered.

"I will set it free far away from here."

Quamar stopped, shrugged. "That will do, too."

When Farad left with the snake. Anna glanced at Quamar. "Will he really use its poison?"

"No," Quamar said. "When you use a knife, the blade must kill instantly. Poison takes too long."

"He didn't want the snake to die." Anna smiled, not surprised. After all, she had observed him tending Morgiana. "Farad is a man who cares for animals."

"And babies, too."

Anna hugged Rashid to her, her mind turning back to the close call they just experienced. "How do mothers do this? Raise a baby in the desert. Raise a child. Protect a child."

"He probably got hot sleeping next to you, Anna. Next time I will keep a closer eye on you and Rashid."

She shook her head. "I could've stopped it from happening."

"You did," Quamar answered. "It was better to find the snake this way and cover him. Vipers tend to hide in the sand if they can't find shade. We were lucky one of us didn't step on him."

Still, Anna couldn't shake the feeling, the ineptness.

"Every child you touch will not end up like Bobby, Anna," Quamar remarked softly.

A high-pitched drone filled the air above their heads.

Quamar shielded his eyes, searched the sky. "Airplane. From the west." He glanced over Anna, noting she wore her scarf. "You don't have your glasses. Here," he said, giving her his pair. "Put these on."

Anna slid them on, then grabbed Rashid. "Come on, handsome, under the robes."

"A search plane will have digital equipment. Lenses. Cameras."

Anna automatically turned her back to the airplane, but her hands fumbled the sling.

"Hurry."

Rashid arched his back and screamed.

"Not now, baby. Please."

Ignoring her plea, Rashid scrunched his face and flung out his hands. With one fist he grabbed the robe, twisting it around his body. "Help me, Quamar."

"I cannot. If they see me put something under your robe, it will draw their attention."

Quamar scanned the area, making a decision. "Anna, we are going to walk to Morgiana. When we get there, put the baby between you and the camel. I will make it look like you are getting ready to ride." He glanced up at the sky. "Hurry."

Quickly, Anna did as he said.

"Rat, hold Morgiana still," Quamar ordered.

Farad grabbed the reigns while Quamar blocked Anna's side and played with the saddle cinch. Anna hunched over slightly and was able to block Rashid's head and body.

"Do not move," Quamar whispered. "Just in case they circle back." He reached for the canteen hanging from Morgiana's saddle. Taking his time, he unscrewed the top and offered some to Anna. "Drink."

After she finished, he drank some himself, then handed the canteen to Farad.

The sun glared down on them, but no one moved. Rashid had even settled in against Anna's stomach. He sucked on his fist and pinched at the camel's hair in front of his nose. "Was it Jarek's plane?"

"I do not know. He has several."

Quamar continued to study the sky.

"What are you thinking?" Anna asked, her eyes following his.

"I am thinking that we should have seen at least a few more reconnaissance planes by now."

"You said the Sahara is vast."

"And it is." Quamar automatically retightened the cinch on Morgiana's saddle. "But the first twenty-four hours, they would estimate our distance and have a much smaller area to cover."

"Yet we've seen only one plane," Anna observed. "And no helicopters or any other vehicles."

"Exactly."

"What does it mean?"

"It means we succeeded in our plans," Quamar reasoned, then patted Morgiana on the neck. "Or they are not concerned about us right now."

"Or we still might have a run-in with them?" Anna asked, already knowing the answer.

"That, too."

ANNA SAT NEXT TO QUAMAR on the rock. After trekking through the sand all day, Quamar called a halt in the early evening, saying they were to wait.

"Rashid is asleep." Anna nodded to where Rashid slept by Farad in the sand, the baby spread-eagled across the little thief's chest. "They're almost inseparable now."

"It is because he smells so pretty."

Anna lifted an eyebrow.

Quamar shrugged. "I have not decided if I trust him yet. He is, after all, a good thief and an even better liar." Quamar studied the blue, cloudless sky. "And he never told me how he got out of that rope when the Al Asheera attacked."

"He told me," Anna answered, unable to contain her smirk. "Morgiana chewed through the rope for him."

"The man can sweet-talk a camel?" Quamar chuckled. "Anyone who can accomplish that would be a good merchant for my father. If I could be sure he would not steal my father's people blind."

"Are we close? To his camp?"

"Yes."

"How do you know?"

"He varies his route every year but stays within the same boundaries of the land. He must when he leads so many. The need for water, grass and food to feed his people—and salt to trade—does not give him many options."

"Won't that fact make it easier for Hassan to locate his camp?"

"Eventually. But it would take weeks."

"What about my father? He could've heard by now of the attack on Taer. He could be sending troops over here as we speak."

"Possibly, but highly unlikely. It might take days for Sandra to reach Roman."

"So we're on our own."

"What makes you say that?" Quamar pointed to the sky. "We always have help."

"Excuse me if I am not as confident in that kind of help as you are. Remember, I've lost two family members waiting for divine intervention."

"God did not kill Bobby and your grandmother, Anna."

"He didn't stop it, either." She sighed. "I don't want to get into a philosophical debate with you, Quamar. So what is the plan for today?"

Quamar saw the paleness of her face, the liquid of her blue eyes. "Do not worry, *Habbibi.* I will protect you."

"That's not what I asked. I did a pretty good job protecting myself and the prince earlier," she commented. "And don't call me your sweetheart again."

"Would you prefer Princess?"

"I would prefer an answer. If we are waiting for your father, how will he contact us?" She pushed the hair from her face. "You expect me to follow you blindly, to risk everything on your word. You demand unconditional trust, yet you risk nothing."

Quamar studied her for a long moment, but Anna refused to take the words back.

"I expect nothing, except what you are willing to give." The fact he was speaking softly did not lessen the anger in his tone. "And I do not risk anything, because I have already lost everything."

Without waiting for a reply, he walked away.

IN THE MORNING BLUR of light and land, a hawk glided in lazy circles, its depthless black eyes keen while taking in the vast territory beneath.

Quamar glanced up at the welcoming cries and watched as the hawk dove over his camp, the gray and white of her wings clearly visible in the semi-light.

"Come and land then," Quamar called, smiling when the bird swooped inches from his head before settling on a nearby boulder. Her wings flapped for a few moments, but from excitement or irritation, Quamar couldn't be sure.

His gaze traveled over the white belly, the grey breast and narrow face of his pet, noting the years had not aged her. He raised his left arm, holding it straight. "Come here, so I can see you better."

The hawk flapped her wings and let out another squawk. This time, Quamar was sure, in irritation. "You are a proud beauty, are you not, Beatrice? And I am sorry I have neglected you for so long."

The hawk's black eyes studied Quamar for several long seconds, as if deciding whether or not to be appeased. After a moment she flew to his arm. But when her feet landed, the sharp talons gripped gently enough not to bite into his skin.

"Another woman you've placated, son. I swear she likes you more than me." The voice came from behind Quamar, but he did not take his attention off the hawk.

"She was mine first, Father. I nursed her back to health when she was young."

Sheik Bari Al Asadi approached from the semidarkness, his camel trailing with slow, plodding steps. "Then you deserted her."

Quamar ignored the censure in his father's tone and, instead, stroked the hawk's breast, rewarding her for not staying angry.

"It's uncanny how she always knows when you are close." Bari dropped the camel's reins and walked toward the fire. He grabbed a cup from nearby and poured himself some tea.

"I have missed you both. Missed home." The truth of the statement caught Quamar off guard.

"Missed or avoided?" Bari questioned with royal derision. Hard-bitten, weathered, Bari was a man who commanded attention from other men. "You cannot return here after years of absence, Quamar, and then expect me to believe you are feeling homesick."

"You sound like a neglected mistress, Father," Quamar mused, before taking a sip of his tea. The sweet, mint taste soothed. And the ache under his heart eased.

Bari answered with an obscenity, leaving Quamar little doubt of his father's opinion. For all his toughness, Bari had a soft heart for his people, for his family.

"You are half-right. I am here because of Taer. Hassan has taken over with the Al Asheera," Quamar said, then murmured a command to Beatrice, who promptly flew back to her perch on the boulder.

"He dares?" Bari stood, his rage shaking his long, lean lines. "With what allies?"

"I do not know. Not yet," Quamar responded, but the promise was there, hardening each syllable. "But I will."

Bari had no doubt that Quamar would fulfill his vow. For Bari understood he had a man for a son. Pride swelled, puffing out his chest a bit. The strength, the integrity was innate. If events had been different, Quamar would have made a good king.

Not one to give in to regrets, Bari asked, "Do you have a plan?"

"Yes," Quamar said. "I have a back door into the palace."

Bari saw the fatigue underlining Quamar's features. The pain that creased his brow. The illness?

"Where is your camp?"

"A few more miles northwest. Against the caves," Bari answered, his mind already running through the implications.

"Good. I have Anna Cambridge and Prince Rashid." Quamar nodded toward the camel.

"I saw them riding in."

"They will be safe with your people."

"Yes," Bari agreed, thoughtfully. "We will need proof to charge Hassan with treason."

"I have the proof and witnesses. One who saw Zahid take Jarek prisoner."

Bari nodded. "We will gather men and leave for Taer tomorrow morning."

"Even with the back door, we need reinforcements, Father. Or it will be a slaughter. Most of Jarek's men have turned traitor. Those loyal were shot. Can you contact Robert Cambridge?"

"It will take time, but I have the means," Bari stated. "Jarek? Saree?"

"Alive," Quamar answered grimly, then stood. It was time to wake the others. "But for how long, I do not know."

Chapter Fifteen

Hassan entered the office with long, angry strides. Jarek had not given in, even after feeling the sting of Zahid's whip.

How could a man endure such a bloody beating? And without a word or a grimace?

Hassan walked to the intercom, then stopped. The rustle of silk, the light fragrance of jasmine filled the air.

"He did not tell you the location of the camp?"

"No, he did not." Hassan glanced surreptitiously at Saree. All signs of the battered woman had disappeared under the jeweled, ivory caftan of a queen. She tapped a fan against her hand with impatience. "A marked improvement on your outfit, Your Highness."

Saree acknowledged his comment with a slight tilt of her head. "And my son?"

"Still with Quamar and the woman."

"Still?" The fan snapped into two. "I'm sure I don't have to remind you, Hassan, that we are running out of time." Saree tossed the broken fan onto the desk. "If you wish to help me rule, we need my son. That is the only way."

Saree detested incompetence. To her, it was nothing more than a lack of breeding. And while Hassan and his contacts had proved effective in the past, she wasn't about to risk failure so close to her goal.

"I have the situation under control."

"We will see." Tempering her anger, she settled herself in the throne chair behind the desk. "Damn that bloody nanny. She was old, but who thought she would be that clever?" She laughed harshly. "And Anna. I had no idea that she had a backbone."

"What has been done can't be changed. We will find Rashid," Hassan replied. "We will find him and return him to his rightful place with you, his mother."

"And then?"

"And then we will kill Jarek and rule in your son's name, of course."

QUAMAR ENTERED HIS TENT, then stopped, surprised.

The tent was larger than most and separated into two sections. In the far section lay a thick layer of tightly weaved rugs, all in various colors, most covered with blue shaded pillows.

Anna lounged between the pillows. Gone were the men's clothes and in their place was a caftan. Long, flowing silk of indigo.

Next to her lay Rashid, bottle in one hand, drinking, while he rocked his small body from side to side. Suddenly, the baby got leverage and flipped over onto his stomach and let out a squeal of delight. Two chubby legs pumped in triumph.

Anna's eyes blinked. "You little monkey." She laughed and hugged the baby before automatically wiping some drool from his smile. "You'd steal my heart if I let you."

"There could be worse sacrifices," Quamar said softly.

Anna stood with the baby. "I'm sorry, I didn't realize…" She stopped her eyes from drinking in his features. "I thought…"

"You thought what, Anna?" He crossed over to her, lured by the hurt in her eyes.

"You had gone to prepare," she answered, then looked down at Rashid. "That you left without saying goodbye."

"We do not leave until the morning." Quamar caught her chin with his finger, brought her gaze back to his. "And I will never leave you without saying goodbye first. I promise."

"Thank you."

He studied her for a moment. "I did not expect to see you here."

"I asked to sleep here. With you gone, I thought I would feel better. Safer."

"And I feel better knowing you are sleeping here." His hand slipped from her chin, curved around her throat, bringing her up and into his chest.

But when his mouth touched hers, it softened so sweetly that Quamar groaned and took the kiss deep.

Faintly, Quamar felt the tap of Rashid's hand against his cheek. He pulled away, took one look at Anna's swollen lips. When he slanted his mouth over her again, Anna curled into his arm.

"Quamar—"

The booming voice was like ice water. Anna jerked from Quamar and scrambled back. Quamar automatically reached out to steady her and the baby.

"Well, now." Bari Al Asadi studied the couple, the flush against the woman's cheeks, his son's scowl. "Well, now," he repeated, not bothering to disguise his pleasure.

"You must be Anna Cambridge." A laugh caught his attention and drew his gaze. Without hesitating he walked over and snagged his grandnephew from Anna and kissed the little boy's forehead. "I came in to see if you and my nephew have eaten."

"Not yet," Quamar answered for Anna, his voice still deep from desire.

"How do you do, Sheik Bari." Recovering, Anna cleared her throat. "We have tea..." She waved in the general direction of the sitting area and smiled.

At six feet tall, Sheik Bari carried his power with ease like his son. Over sixty, his once thick, black hair had long ago turned silver, accenting the dark pitch of his eyes. Hard-earned crevices mapped his face, the result of years spent outdoors in the unforgiving elements.

"Miss Cambridge—"

"Please, call me Anna."

"Very well. Anna." Bari glanced from his son to the woman. "Quamar, the men require your help with the weapons and provisions."

"I will be there in a minute—"

"I believe they need you now."

Quamar lifted an eyebrow, seeing the dismissal for what it was. "Very well." But his tone was anything but pleased.

He turned to Anna. "I will see you later this evening." With a warning glance to her, he salaamed his father and left the tent in long, quick strides.

"Sheik Bari, I am sorry—"

The sheik put up a hand, effectively cutting off Anna's apology. "No need to be. He is, after all, my son." Bari noticed the tea and biscuits sitting nearby on the mat. "Come, Anna, join me for a few minutes. I have an important request to make."

Bari sat on the floor and immediately gave Rashid a hard, round, oat biscuit to chew on. "Quamar has his mother's temperament."

"Only his mother's?" Anna asked, unable to contain her grin. Rashid crawled into her lap, bits of mushy biscuit on his cheeks. Gently, Anna brushed them off.

Bari laughed, a deep low chuckle that was warm, rough. Like an old wool blanket.

"Did you know that your father and I are friends, Anna?"

"No. I didn't." It wasn't the words, but the serious tone that had her glancing up from the baby. After all, her father had many acquaintances.

"In fact, I was the one that brought Jarek and Robert together for this oil deal," he acknowledged after a moment. "While we honor our traditions, Taer has lived too long in the past."

"I don't understand how this—"

"Has Quamar told you about his injury? That

he is dying?" Bari asked, his dark eyes boring into hers.

"Yes," she said quietly.

"I thought so," Bari said, grimly. He stroked his beard for a moment. "Only I and Sandra Haddad know. And now you."

"I didn't give him much choice," Anna murmured.

Bari's eyebrow rose. "If he didn't want you to know, he would never have told you."

Rashid waved his half-eaten biscuit in front of her face. Happy for the brief distraction, she pretended to eat it until Rashid laughed.

"Did he tell you that he had the option of surgery to prevent his death?"

Anna stiffened; her eyes shot to Bari's. "No."

"There is a high risk he would come out of the surgery lobotomized. Leaving him a vegetable. Because of this, he will not have the surgery. To him, he would be neither dead nor living."

"And you think I might be able to persuade him to have the surgery?" Anna asked. "When he didn't even tell me that surgery was an option?" The hurt was there, underlining her words.

"I love my son, Anna. The only person I loved as much was my beautiful Theresa. I have lived many years without her and many years worrying if I would have to live without my son. You cannot blame me for trying to save his life. Even if in his stubbornness, he refuses to save it himself."

"If you think I could change his mind—" Anna shook her head "—you are wrong. As I said, he didn't even tell me about the surgery."

"Possibly," Bari said. "It would not be the first time I have made a mistake."

Anna studied the older man for a moment. "Why do you think he would listen to me?"

"He loves you," Bari said softly. "And if I'm not mistaken, you love him, too."

Suddenly, Bari stood and scooped Rashid into his arms. "Do not give up on my son, Anna, like he has given up on himself. You may be his last hope."

"PRINCESS?"

Anna stepped out of the tent when she heard Farad.

The little man rushed up to her, a grin on his face. "Sheik Bari has offered me a position among his people as one of his merchant traders." Farad's chest puffed out with pride. "The salt they barter has not brought them in enough supplies. Master Quamar suggested that I could help, and Sheik Bari agreed."

Anna hugged her friend. "I'm happy for you. So you are staying on?"

"Oh, yes." He nodded. "First I will help them defeat Hassan, then I will come back here to live."

"You like Sheik Bari, don't you?"

"I would have liked him as our king."

Startled, Anna glanced at Farad.

"Bari was next in line to be king of Taer?"

"He abdicated his throne," Farad explained. "After Bari met Theresa Bazan, Bari's father forbade the relationship. You see, not only was she Italian but she was a Christian. And at the time, such a marriage was forbidden."

"So what happened?"

"Sheik Bari refused to give up Theresa Bazan and abdicated. His throne went to the middle son, Makrad."

"Jarek's father."

"Yes, Hassan is the youngest of the three. Some say he worshiped Sheik Bari until he abdicated. Now the brothers do not talk."

"And Jarek's parents died last year."

"Yes, in an auto accident. Just after the announcement that Queen Saree was expecting."

"So Quamar would've been king, if Bari had not abdicated?"

"No," Farad answered, surprise in his voice. "Master Quamar is a bastard and has no right to the crown. Bari would not marry any other after falling in love with Theresa Bazan. If Bari had remained king and died, the throne still went to Makrad and then to Jarek."

"Bari and Theresa never married?"

"No," Farad answered, confused. "I thought you understood. Bari could not marry a Christian. But they lived together as man and wife in all other ways. Something he could not have done as king."

"Quamar grew up with this over him," Anna commented. "I didn't realize stigmas like that still existed in the world." But she understood now. Quamar had grown up loved but always considered a bastard.

Anna's heart hurt for the little boy who was Quamar. Family meant everything to him, because he never truly belonged.

And if you didn't belong, why not die alone?

Anna observed the encampment. Children played while others were being taught. Most of the women gathered sand in their baskets. One by one they dumped each basket in the middle of camp. Others smoothed out the sand, creating a flat hill.

"What are they doing, Farad?"

"They are getting ready for the *Tafca,* the war dance. The men leave in the morning for the palace and war. So they celebrate tonight."

"They're having a party?"

"Bari believes in the old ways. That is one reason why the people love him," Farad admitted. "It's our way of asking for Allah's blessing and showing him how much we appreciate our life. When a person goes to war, it's to protect what we cherish most. It should be celebrated, don't you think?"

"I don't know what to think, honestly," Anna responded. All her life she'd fought against death. The idea of celebrating before the possibility meant one had to accept the possibility.

"The women will wear their veils and skirts. And dance to the beat of drums. During this time, it is tradition for young lovers to declare themselves. They believe those who are in love will be graced with Allah's protection. And have a better chance of returning unharmed. And if they don't, they will die with their loved ones on their minds and in their hearts."

Anna's gaze drifted over to Quamar. He stood a head above Bari's men—his profile edged with grim determination, his broad shoulders set with the innate strength of a man.

Suddenly, he captured her eyes with his—the pitch-black irises now cool, distant.

A heartbeat later, they shifted away.

Farad followed the exchange, saw the heartache, the sheen of tears in his princess's eyes.

Anna lifted her chin, stiffened her spine. "Farad, will you help me with something?" Her voice was pitched low, but resolute.

He understood immediately. Who could not, when her face reflected her heart? "Yes, Princess. I will."

Chapter Sixteen

The slow, rhythmic beat of drums filled the night air. Its tempo prodded some to dance while others clapped and laughed, enjoying the music from a distance.

Quamar sat on the outer rim of the sandy platform with his father, lost in thought.

He had hurt Anna today. On purpose. Hurt them both as a reminder of what could happen if they took their relationship any further.

Deliberately, he kept himself busy far into the evening. Not wanting proximity to weaken his resolve. Each time he got close to Anna his control slipped.

He and his father had decided it was safest to leave her at camp. Another reason he hadn't seen her today. She would not like the news, and he wished to put it off as long as possible.

"Watch, Quamar," his father prodded. "The

women are going to dance." A hush settled over the camp while the drums pounded a slow, steady rhythm.

Quamar glanced up just as Anna stepped from his tent, dressed in the more traditional clothes of his people.

Her hair had been left hanging straight, covered with a thin, almost transparent silk veil.

Indigo. His father's tribal color.

His color.

Another scarf, just as frail, draped the lower part of her face. Passion darkened her eyes to azure-blue—wickedly enhanced by deep, smoky black kohl and pitch-black lashes.

Sequins flashed in the firelight, drawing his gaze to her sleeveless vest. With every movement, the whisper-thin fabric stretched and clung to the curves of her breasts.

Unable to stop himself, he followed the line of her body, skimming over the bare midriff, the gentle slope of her waist.

A matching silk skirt draped her hips, leaving skin exposed beneath her navel, her bare feet visible below the hem.

A fever ignited within him, flowing through his veins. Beating it back, he forced his eyes to the horizon, using the twilight to distract him.

But each drumbeat pulsated through him. Taunting him.

Against his will, his gaze slid back. Her laughter, low but triumphant, reached him, telling him he'd lost one battle.

She wore tribal bands of gold high on her upper arms. They glinted in the firelight, drawing his gaze as she moved with the music. Stiff at first, she soon was joined by other women, all dancing for their men. The sway of their hips, the gentle movement of their torsos, each set of eyes on one man, their man.

His blood thickened, then pooled in his loins. Grinding his teeth, Quamar swore.

Leisurely, Anna moved in front of him, leaving no doubt to anyone watching who she danced for. Her hands skimmed her hips, brushing the low waistband of her skirt, hanging for a long second, before her fingers slid to the bare skin of her waist, the sides of her breasts.

Quamar tightened his muscles. When she lifted her hair, exposing the long, slim curve of her neck, desire whipped through him, making him weak. Making him want.

For a moment, she stayed suspended, waiting until she had his full attention. When his gaze locked onto her, onyx clashed against azure.

Slowly, the strands slipped through her fingers, only to flow once again over her shoulders.

He released his breath in one long hiss.

With arms above her head, she moved in a small circle. The firelight cast shadows and light against her body, until she became the exotic creature that haunted his dreams.

The tempo increased and Anna laughed again, a low, husky laugh meant to tempt. Her hips gyrated easily now, keeping the beat. She drifted to him until they were mere inches apart. This close, he caught her scent. Sultry, female.

Excitement flushed her skin, had her muscles quivering. With one slow finger, she trailed a line from the throbbing pulse at the base of his neck to the tight line of his lips.

Quamar fisted his hands, struggled not to touch her back.

For a second she hovered close, her lips a mere breath away from his.

"No, Anna," he whispered, but the words crackled with desperation.

Suddenly she circled back to the women, smiling with female satisfaction.

"You can say no to that, my son?"

"What?" Quamar, wound tight, nearly shouted the question, forgetting his father sat beside him.

Bari chuckled, bouncing Rashid in his lap.

"I have no choice."

"Bah!" Bari snorted. "Do not talk to me about choices." He watched Anna with two other women, laughing and spinning. "She has courage, like your mother. Are you in love with her?"

"Yes, but that changes nothing."

The music stopped. In the silence Anna faced Quamar, her breath rapid, her body flushed, her eyes wide with excitement.

"There is always a choice. People make them every minute of every day." Bari tickled Rashid under his chin.

Quamar glared at his father. "What are you trying to say?"

"Maybe it's time to choose for the minute," Bari suggested. "Not for the day."

When Quamar glanced back, Anna was gone.

MUSIC AND LAUGHTER DRIFTED through the gaps in the tent. Restless, Anna paced, trying to calm the nerves that still throbbed beneath the pink flush of her skin. It was her own driving passion that surprised her. The primitive, almost decadent behavior had been like a drug. It was as if every nerve in her body screamed, urging her to move, to tempt.

Agitated, Anna grasped her veil to pull it free, then hesitated. Doubts assailed her, but she pushed them away and with them, pride, trepidation.

She loved him. And he would go to war tomorrow.

It was enough for tonight.

Leaving the veil in place, she struck a match to light a nearby candle. With the dancing, she had enticed, summoned.

Heat prickled the back of her neck. Before she even turned around, she knew he was there, watching, waiting.

He had obeyed.

Gone were the robes, the turban. His linen shirt hung loose and open, fastened with only the last two buttons. The way, she had learned, he preferred.

Never before had he looked more like a warrior. His stance was wide, his features set in granite and void of emotion. His black irises remained hooded, but beneath they glittered, sharp with desire, need.

The prickling skittered down her spine, invaded her belly then lower, until she ached. Without a word, she lit the candle and blew out the match.

A dim hue filled the tent, bringing with it the intimacy she wanted.

"Rashid?" he asked, his voice rough. Sandpaper against his vocal cords.

She found the harshness comforting, calming. "With your father for the night."

He nodded once, but didn't come forward. Silence surrounded them. Enough that she could almost hear his heart beating, feel his pulse hitch, both matching the erratic rhythm of her own.

"I will leave you, Anna," he whispered.

"I know." She smiled, trying to reassure him, to offset the sadness underlining her words. "But not tonight."

With slow, deliberate steps, he came for her. Giving her another unspoken opportunity to change her mind.

As her smile deepened, she met him halfway until only inches separated them. "What took you so long?" Her heart pounded against her ribs. Unable to stop, her fingers traced a light path from his stomach to his chest. Muscle and warm skin flexed then smoothed beneath her touch.

Still, he said nothing. But when his hand rose and cupped her cheek, his fingers trembled.

If she hadn't loved him already, she would've fallen then.

He tugged the veil free, allowing his gaze to roam her face. Heavy lidded, her eyes darkened with passion, holding her in place, stealing her breath.

"*Roh albi wa hayati wa habibi.* You are my soul and my heart and my love, Anna." With a groan, his mouth settled possessively over hers.

Suddenly desperate to close what little space remained, she gripped his shoulders, bringing him to her. His tongue eased into her mouth, stroking, rubbing against hers, coaxing until she responded with wild abandon.

Vaguely, she felt a tug at her hair, realized the veil had broken free. Delicious shivers slipped through her as the soft material skimmed her shoulder, her neck, then slipped away to pool on the floor.

His fingers buried themselves in the thick strands of her hair. Twining, stroking. With a growl, he pulled back, tasted the sweet curve of her jaw. "So beautiful. I could not bear the thought of your hair being cut by Elizabeth."

His teeth caught her earlobe, nibbled until she whimpered with pleasure, then he continued his assault on her jaw, her throat, her collarbone. Her chest rubbed restlessly against his, her fingers digging into the hard, sinewy shoulders. "Quamar, please." Her breasts tingled, her nipples tightened in anticipation.

He laughed wickedly against the sensitive hollow of her neck, raising goose bumps across her shoulders, down her back.

With a flick of his fingers, her vest opened, exposing her to his heated gaze.

Suddenly, Quamar dropped to his knees in

front of her, gathered her close, pressing his lips to her belly. His mouth was hot against her skin. He nibbled, tasting the lines and curves of her hips, her ribs.

When his teeth closed over her breast, Anna whimpered, then groaned. Blood raced from her head, pooled between her legs. Her knees weakened and would have collapsed but Quamar tightened his hold. Gently, he suckled, circled and rubbed with his tongue until her head lolled back, her fingers dug in.

Another tug and her skirt joined the veils at her feet. A hiss of his breath told her he'd found out she wore nothing underneath.

"Surprise," she rasped. The air caressed her nakedness, cooling her skin, giving her back some strength.

She leaned into him, gasping when her nipples brushed his cheek. She tugged his shirt apart, not caring when buttons popped.

Slowly, she slipped the material down the slopes of his shoulders, over the tight biceps and forearms, enjoying the power she held beneath her touch. The shirt hit the floor with her sigh.

Without warning, Quamar slid his arms under her legs, lifted her against his chest and carried her to his bed.

As he set her down, she came to her knees, pausing until the heat of his gaze slid over her. With a dip of her shoulders, she shrugged off the vest.

Quamar savored the moment, spellbound. Her blond hair curled wildly about her shoulders, mussed from his hands, the ends touching her breasts just above each hardened nipple.

He was hard and hot. His body throbbed with the need to be inside her, to feel her damp softness surround him.

The blue of her eyes deepened to pools of indigo. Swirling with passion, they beckoned him closer. Resisting, his gaze swept over her body, perfectly formed with high, taut breasts, soft feminine curves and alabaster skin now flushed with passion.

Quickly he finished stripping. When she raised her arms, he gathered her close. Anna kissed his shoulder, his jaw, his scar. He smelled of the wind and the desert.

"Anna, I need…" She looked at him when he hesitated. The power was there, in his limbs, in his torso. He was a warrior first, foremost. Unable to stop, her gaze drifted down. He was full, hard and…

Her eyes shot back to his, widening. "Quamar, I don't think we'll…will we? I mean—"

His kiss cut her off before she could finish. His tongue swept inside to mate with hers.

Then with amazing gentleness, he laid her back, covered her body with his own. "We will fit," he whispered, smiling against her ear, his breath moist. He nibbled the lobe, then soothed it with his tongue.

Her moans of pleasure drove him back to the edge.

Growling, he slipped his hips between her thighs until she cradled his hardness. "I am asking you, Anna Cambridge," he murmured, his breath now hot against the hollow of her jaw. "Will you take me…all of me…for tonight? To have and to hold until the dawn rises once more?"

"I will," she whispered, not bothering to check the single tear that rolled down her temple. Although her heart ached with the request, she wouldn't beg him to stay past the morning. Wouldn't force him to choose. If this was all they had, so be it.

With a sigh, he gripped her hips, bringing her forward. Slowly, he pressed into her soft folds, letting out a ragged groan when her body yielded—moist and warm.

"That's right, *Habbibi,* relax." He pushed a little deeper, growling as she slid like hot silk across the tight skin of his shaft, taking satisfaction in the delicate shivers that rippled through her body.

With one hand he stroked her belly, caressing the tense muscles beneath. Anna lifted her hips, instinctively pushing upward against him. He was big, but her loins throbbed, clenched, then stretched to accept.

"More, Anna," Quamar pleaded, his voice strained, his features carved in exquisite pain. A thin sheen of perspiration covered his brow.

Anna barely noticed. White-hot desire balled deep in her belly. She arched again, allowing him to sink deeper into her. Quamar reared back, and the cords of his neck stood out, straining from his fight for control. "Almost, baby. Just a little—" Anna whimpered, wanting more, her body more than willing—needing the relief he could only bring.

"Quamar, please!" she demanded, the need almost unbearable.

He took a shuddering breath, tried to be gentle, but she wouldn't let him. Instead, she dug her nails into his shoulders, grasping him closer.

Both of them were panting now, neither getting enough oxygen. Tiny shocks exploded through Anna's limbs, making them shake with desire.

With one hard thrust, he sheathed to the hilt, taking them both to the precipice of their passion.

His hands found hers, pushed them down to the pillow by her head, each finger threaded between hers. This was where he belonged, this was where he could stay for the rest of his days. The muscles on his lower back tightened, fighting for release.

Her thin cry of frustration filled the air between them. "Let go, I will catch you," he murmured. His thrusts deepened, grew faster. *I will love you,* he breathed silently with each stroke. Protecting himself, protecting her by not saying the words out loud.

Flushed from exertion, her legs quivered around him, causing him to take deep ragged breaths. *I love you.* The words ran through his mind, until they became a prayer.

Anna strained for release, caught in a desperate fever, fighting a battle with Quamar's assault on her body.

On the next stroke he pushed deep, his body throbbing within, the sweet intensity causing him to rear back, clench his jaw. But he did not let go of her hands.

With a soft sob, Anna shattered with pleasure, her body liquefying even as Quamar flexed, strained, then convulsed with his own release, pouring himself into her.

When it was over, Quamar started shifting away, but Anna reached out to stop him. "Not yet," she whispered, not wanting to feel the emptiness he would leave in her when he withdrew.

He eased back. But instead of bracing himself above her, he brought her with him as he rolled onto his back, keeping himself buried within her.

Her soft sigh stirred against his chest. “I love you, Quamar.”

And he was lost.

Chapter Seventeen

As dawn broke over the Sahara, Quamar struggled for the distance that had once been second nature to him. For so many reasons, the secrets of his job, the risk of others' lives.

But Anna's sigh, her words, haunted him. Enough to drive him out of her arms and into the morning chill. Women had said they loved him before. For many reasons. To persuade, to deceive, in the throes of passion. They had become words for the casual.

But not Anna. Quamar understood that Anna had not given her love to anyone since the death of Bobby.

He would protect her, then walk away. And in doing so, cut both their hearts out.

"You were going to leave without saying goodbye." It was a statement, not a question.

Quamar turned. She stood with his robe

wrapped around her, a scarf hooding her hair, leaving only her features visible. His heart ached to have her.

Twice more he had turned to her in the night, the last time in a savage need that had left them both exhausted but sated.

Quamar shook his head. "No." He looked to the horizon. "No matter how hard, I will say goodbye."

She stepped up to him, raised a hand to his cheek. "And will it be hard?"

Quamar covered her hand with his own. "Yes," he rasped.

"Then don't say it," she whispered. "Say you love me instead. Say no matter what, we will fight it together."

"I cannot," he answered in a ragged breath. He was a man being stretched on a rack.

With a groan, he covered her mouth with his, taking her sweet lips in a deep, lingering kiss. It would be the last time.

When he broke away, they both fought for breath. He tilted her chin up until their eyes met. "Anna, promise me you will find someone else to love. Live the life you were meant to live."

"No." She smiled sadly, the sheen of tears making the blue of her eyes shine in the morning light. "I told you before, I won't make promises I can't keep."

In the stillness of the dawn, a hawk's cry broke into their words—a cry of warning.

Quamar searched the sand, the rocks, their shadows until he caught a glimpse of crimson against stone.

"The Al Asheera."

"Here?"

How they'd come so quickly, he'd leave to sort out when the time allowed.

"Go, find Rashid. Take the women and children to the caves. I need to warn my father."

THEY CAME DOWN from the hills, most on foot, others in machine-gun-mounted jeeps. Their trilling echoed off the canyon walls. Not for warning, but to put fear into the hearts of their victims.

The Al Asheera maneuvered swifter, hid better on their feet.

Most carried swords, while others held rifles and spears. They didn't overrun, knowing the men would stand and fight. Instead they made passes, coming with a rush of bullets, then disappearing in the banks of sand dunes, only to reappear moments later.

Bari understood war—he'd been a soldier too long. Most of his men had guns, for he was what he was—royalty. And with royalty came the need to protect. Those that had rifles had been trained to use them.

"Anna?"

"With the women," Bari replied, his hand gripping his son's shoulder. "She is safe for now."

Before Quamar could reply, an Asheera charged him from a boulder. Quamar fired, saw the dust jump from the enemy's robe when the bullet hit.

Volleys of bullets strafed the ground, pushing Bari's people back behind the rocks and shrubs.

"Aim for the machine guns!" Quamar screamed over the cries of the wounded and dying. Still, when one of Bari's men fell, another was there to take his place. "Wait for the shot. Don't waste your ammunition."

Quamar was everywhere, encouraging, shooting, keeping those who wanted to bolt standing their ground.

The second rush ended. The desert once again empty of the living. Scattered over the sand lay the dead. Some from the first rush were already covered with an inch of sand.

Someone howled in pain. Another coughed. In the distance, Quamar could hear some women crying with their children. He took comfort from the sound, knowing they were alive.

While some of the Taer men had died, more lay wounded. The Al Asheera pulled back, this time for cover among the rock and dunes. They were men who lived for desert battles, for war.

And they had patience.

"FARAD!" ANNA RAN through the camp, dodging the women who were already packing supplies while others corralled the children. All getting ready for the short hike to the cave just beyond the tents.

"Princess!" Farad's voice came from inside Quamar's tent.

She jerked back the flap and stopped. "Farad. Thank goodness," she said with relief. Rashid sat in the baby sling across Farad's stomach. "We are under attack. We must get the women and children to the caves." Automatically she reached for Rashid.

A knife ripped through the back of the tent. Before Anna could react, Zahid stepped through holding a rifle. He pointed it at Rashid and Farad. "Going somewhere?"

AN HOUR GREW into two. The sun gained momentum, broiling the earth beneath. Heat pressed down on them, sucking the oxygen from the air, until each breath left their lungs burning. But the sweat-soaked Taerians held their posts, clasping the metal rifles now firebrand-hot from that same sun.

Occasionally a gun barked from the camp, and

if they were lucky, an answering scream erupted from the desert sand. The shrill cry broke the silence of the dead Al Asheera that lay scattered among the rocks.

Instinct told Quamar that the Al Asheera were moving, taking their time, slithering through the sand, using brush and rocks, their dead, for concealment.

The next attack would be closer, less than fifty meters. A narrow margin of distance gave the camp's more experienced gunmen a chance for one, maybe two shots before they were over-run. It would be the Al Asheera's final assault. The intent—to overrun, to demolish.

Having made the same determination as his son, Bari worked his way through the line of men, ordering them in low murmurs to be ready.

Dust rose with the wind, clogging nostrils, stinging eyes. He patted those on the back who needed the comfort, hardened his voice for the ones who still struggled for courage. All the while he told them to keep their guns leveled, their gazes sharp for movements.

Quamar shifted. He'd been here before. Too many times to count. Something tightened inside him. Anger maybe, certainly fear. The stakes had never been this high. Anna had changed that.

Suddenly, the Al Asheera rose from the sand, bloodred vipers raising their heads to strike.

"Get ready!" Quamar's command cracked like a cannon over their heads. "Hold your ground, if for nothing else, then for your families. We are the only wall standing between them and your enemy."

The men flanked the Al Asheera, forming a curved line of defense. A chance to attack their enemy from all sides. A small chance, Quamar thought grimly.

Suddenly, gunfire rung out. But this time from behind the Al Asheera lines.

Two military dune buggies rose over the crest—both equipped with rapid-fire machine guns mounted on the roll bars. Two men were positioned in each vehicle. One driving, one shooting, all four dressed in desert camouflage.

Bari's men fired, catching the Al Asheera in a cross fire of bullets. Within seconds, their enemy's advance broke. Al Asheera scattered, trying to defend themselves from both flanks, knowing as they fought they would be massacred.

Just as suddenly as the attack had started, it was done. Those Al Asheera who survived were rounded up by Bari's men. A cheer rose from the camp, followed by random rifle shots. They had won.

Quamar walked out to meet the two dune buggies.

"Heard you needed some help."

Quamar grinned, recognizing the raven-black hair, lean aristocratic features, the tempered gray eyes beneath the dust and grime. Dressed in full military gear, Cain MacAlister—the director of Labyrinth—approached Quamar, his hand extended. Quamar grasped the hand, pulled Cain into a bear hug.

"So, where's the beer?" Ian MacAlister added from a few feet away. Quamar let go of Cain and slapped Ian on the shoulder. Unlike his brother, Ian was meat and muscle, his features more pretty than masculine.

"You look like hell, friend."

Quamar swung around at the comment as the other two men jumped from their vehicle.

Quamar clasped the hand of his best friend. A full-blown Italian with the chiseled features of his ancestors, Roman D'Amato was quick to temper, but even quicker to humor.

"In the nick of time mean anything to you, Cerberus?" Quamar intentionally used Roman's Labyrinth code name, even though his friend had retired from the agency long before. After marrying Ian and Cain's sister, Kate.

"Hell, Quamar, you're bloody lucky we got

here at all." Jordan Beck answered the question. The last of the four, Jordan was the only field agent still working for Labyrinth. Quamar took in the lanky body, the sharp British features that now sported a good three days of whiskers. "The fact that President Cambridge wants his daughter back made it a little easier," Jordan continued. He rubbed the side of his nose. "This isn't exactly our war, now is it, mate?"

Quamar looked at Roman. "Sandra contacted you?"

"Yes," Roman responded. "Whoever she is, she's one brave lady."

"She is an old friend. And yes, she is brave," Quamar agreed, then took Ian and Cain in with one glance. "Did you bring some of your toys?"

"If you mean things like acid rope, laser cutters and some plastic explosives—" Ian grinned "—oh, yeah. Kate sends her love." Kate MacAlister D'Amato was not only Ian and Cain's sister, she also happened to be head of Labyrinth's technical division.

"Good." Quamar nodded. "We have a palace to take back."

"The five of us?" Ian questioned, his eyebrows drawn.

"I'm in if it's for king and country." Jordan smiled good-naturedly. "Besides, I like the odds.

Hate too many people underfoot. End up tripping over them. With the five of us, I won't have to worry about who I'm shooting at."

"Just don't shoot any innocents," Cain remarked.

"Quamar." Bari approached, his steps quick, impatient. He nodded to the men, but waved off any introduction. Instead he turned to his son. "It's Anna. The Al Asheera have her. They have them both. Rashid was with her."

"How?"

"The tent."

Quamar immediately changed directions, his pace picking up speed as he got closer to the tent. Panic had him ripping open the flap, running in. The back wall flapped in the breeze, the material sliced from floor to ceiling.

Bari followed him in. "We have no idea how long they've had her. Could have been as early as the initial strike against us."

Quamar shoved his way out through the damaged tent, fear in every step. He crouched, studied the ground. "There were more than one. At least three."

The hawk's shadow passed over the footprints. Quamar looked to the sky. Beatrice circled in large loops, swooping only to pull again to the heights, keeping her distance.

"Something's wrong," Roman noted. "Otherwise she would land. Right?"

"Yes," Quamar answered, his eyes already searching the horizon. "We need to follow her."

Cain let out a shrill whistle. Within moments they were joined by Jordan, Roman and Ian. "Spread out," he ordered. "Three shots."

It took them ten minutes to reach Beatrice, each adding a year to Quamar's life.

What he saw made his stomach sicken. Farad had been stripped to his linen pants and staked spread-eagle on the ground.

Roman snagged his pistol and fired three shots into the air, signaling to the others that they had found him.

"This is Zahid's handiwork," Quamar said and pointed to the horsewhip marks on Farad's chest. Crisscrossed from shoulder to hip, raw skin oozed blood, flayed open to burn in the sun's heat.

Quamar crouched, laid his finger against Farad's throat. "He's still alive."

One by one, Roman slit Farad's bonds. "From the sunburn on his face, I'd say he's been out here for at least two hours." His eyes scanned the immediate area. "Zahid is long gone by now."

"I want to get him back to the tents, then we can figure out what the hell happened." Quamar lifted Farad, cradling him.

Roman caught the underlying fear in Quamar's statement. The dark eyes sharpened on his friend. "Is Anna personal? Or political?"

"Personal," Quamar responded, eating the ground up in long, quick strides.

When they approached the camp, they found the others waiting.

Ian took one look at the little man and whistled between his teeth.

Farad's eyes fluttered open. "Master Quamar…Zahid…"

Quamar entered his tent, then laid the thief on his bed.

"Zahid took her and the baby, just before the attack. I tried to stop him—"

"We know," Quamar answered. "But how did he find her?"

"I'd made a deal," Farad admitted. "But I broke it, the morning we fought the Al Asheera. It was the princess, she was so kind, I couldn't…"

"If you broke the deal, how did he find her, Farad?" Quamar questioned.

"Zahid told me one of his soldiers had placed a homing device in my money pouch, under the seam. I led him to you all without realizing it."

Quamar stood, his hands fisted.

"I didn't know, Master Quamar. I swear."

Quamar sighed. "I believe you, Farad."

"Looks like we're heading to the palace." Ian handed the thief an open canteen, watched him drink for a moment.

Farad jerked the canteen from his mouth. "Take me with you."

"You aren't in any condition—"

Farad sat up, grimaced but did not cry out. "I am strong enough to get you into the palace without being seen."

Ian raised an eyebrow. "And how is that, little man?"

"The sewers."

Jordan swore. "How did I know he would say something like that?"

Chapter Eighteen

Anna paced the suite. It had been four hours since she'd been left there. Four hours since Zahid had taken Rashid away from her.

Frustrated, she glanced around the bedroom. The white Persian rugs, the gray marble tile with matching gray curtains and coverlet—all made of satin, all adorning burnt red cherrywood furniture. And all useless.

She'd spent the first hour looking for a weapon, the next two for a means of escape—only to come up with nothing.

Anna glanced down at the suitcase, open on the bed, with dresses and blouses carelessly tossed to the side.

Even her phone had gone missing.

"Looking for your cell?"

Anna glanced up into the bureau mirror. Behind her a woman stood in the doorway, dressed in a caftan of ivory, trimmed with jewels, her long black hair swept back from her face. With one hand she waved the guard away. With the other she held Rashid.

"Saree?" Anna swung around, facing her friend. When she glanced down, she saw Rashid held her cell to his mouth, chewing on the end as if it were a teething ring.

"Hello, darling."

"Saree." Anna whispered the words. "I thought…we thought—"

"That Hassan had killed me?" Saree laughed as she walked toward the bed. "No, dear. Hassan *helped* me." She stepped past Anna and patted her face. "You see, I'm going to rule Taer with my son."

"But Hassan—"

"You don't think *he* had the power to pull off this little rebellion, do you?"

Anna frowned in disbelief.

"You *did*." Saree's mouth pouted with sympathy. "My, you are simple."

"If Hassan wanted to rule, why didn't he kill Rashid?" Anna said, still trying to understand.

"He couldn't be that obvious." Saree glanced over her shoulder. "Could he, Zahid?"

"My father has kept a low profile, as you Americans say." Zahid stood at the doorway, his shoulder against the pane, his whip tapping his palm. "The Al Asheera believed it is I alone involved in their cause. They are wrong and soon will be driven out. With some help from our neighbors."

"A neighbor that is willing to pay a lot more for our oil than your daddy, Anna," Saree inserted.

"Our neighbor has offered to help stop the revolution. If by some chance, I am incriminated..." With his hand resting on his sword, he salaamed toward Saree. "I will be pardoned by my lovely Queen."

"As you should be," Saree responded easily.

"I never wanted power, Miss Cambridge. Only profit." He straightened and smiled. "And Jarek dead."

"You won't succeed." Stunned and sickened, Anna whispered the words.

"But, darling, I already have," Saree said, then tickled Rashid's cheek. "It was unfortunate that Alma gave you Rashid. The plan had been to kill you and Jarek right away."

"Me?"

"Yes, you, darling. Why did you think I invited you here?" Saree laughed. "You are the bonus, Anna. You are what clinched the deal. Killing you will be the tragedy that will break the oil deal with the United States. It wasn't our fault you died. But bad feelings will strain the negotiations." She paused, smiling. "I'm sure of it."

"I thought Alma gave me Rashid because she couldn't find you," Anna said. "But the truth was, she didn't trust you. Isn't it?"

"Yes, well, she was old, but not stupid," Saree admitted. "And loyal to my husband."

Anna's head jerked up. "I really thought that our friendship—"

"It wasn't all fake, Anna. I found you somewhat amusing. But most of the time, yes, it was a chore. But one I was willing to deal with. You have to admit being friends with the daughter of one the most powerful men in the world had its advantages."

Anna swallowed back the bile that rose to her throat. So many people dead.

"Oh, by the way." She started for the door. "Zahid gets *you,* too." She paused when she reached Zahid, shifting Rashid to her other arm. "Meet me in my office when you are through here. We still have loose ends to tie up, now that Bari's people are dead."

"ALL RIGHT, GENTLEMEN, who goes first?" Ian asked the question as all five men eyed the brick well in the ground. Ian glanced at Quamar. "Looks like it might be a tight squeeze for you, big guy."

"I will fit." Quamar stepped forward, handed his backpack to Ian and then bit down on a small flashlight. "Just make sure you do not fall on me."

"Please hurry." Farad glanced around nervously, not used to being in the middle of a group of such large men. "If someone should see us..."

"How far is the drop, Rat?" Quamar used his arms to keep himself balanced in the tube.

"Three meters. Maybe four. No more. Be careful, it angles."

"Think of a big slide, Quamar," Jordan commented wryly.

Quamar grunted and slid down the tube feet-first. Immediately water surrounded him, coming up to his knees and soaking his boots. He stepped out of the way and hit the switch on his flashlight. Made of mortar and bricks, the walls seemed to move with the light. Quamar saw cockroaches scatter, while others rained down on his head.

Quamar waded farther in to give the others room. Rats squealed, sending more bugs scurrying.

"Looks like we're not alone down here," Roman said from behind him. Cain came next, followed by Jordan, then Ian.

Farad came last, not making a comment when the water hit him mid-thigh. "Follow me. Quickly. As we get closer to the city there will be more visibility."

The tunnel of bricks was no more than five feet high, less with the sludge that caked the ground beneath their feet.

"These sewers are over two hundred years old." Farad had little trouble tramping through at full height. The five agents had to bend almost completely at the waist to get through the tunnel.

"Overhead." Quamar pointed to where the crown of the tunnel bowed from old age, reducing the height by another six inches in some places. "Watch your scalp."

Sand sifted through the cracks where mortar had broken away. The heat from the ground drove the temperature of the sewer well over a hundred degrees, thickening the air into fetid syrup.

"Walk with the flow," Farad suggested. "It keeps the water from splashing into your faces."

"Trust me, we've dealt with worse," Ian muttered. "But I retired to get out of the crap jobs. Literally."

Farad pointed to smaller tubes coming from the top of the crown. "Be careful. Those side pipes are connected to various bathrooms and other networks of tubes."

"Just great," Ian complained. "You're saying those are privy tubes."

"Yes. And laundry or kitchen." The men moved

quietly through the maze, following Farad without question. Suddenly the little man stopped and pointed up. "Here."

Above their heads was a cylinder nearly a foot in diameter. "This leads to the king's cell. It is his privy. A hole in the floor."

"You use those to get into the palace?" Jordan remarked, studying the drain. "Clever begger, aren't you?"

Cain gauged the width. "We can't fit up there."

"I can free him," said Farad. From his pouch he produced a set of picks. "You can use another and meet me at his cell."

He waved the men to follow him five more feet to a bigger tube, one the width of the men's shoulders. "This leads to the bathroom by the cells. It's for all the men to use. Communal. But they covered it years ago with a sheet of steel."

"No problem." Ian reached into his pack, pulled out an acid rope.

Quamar turned to Farad. "We'll give you a five-minute head start. Don't waste it."

"I usually have to climb myself. But if you boost me up, it will save me time."

Quamar locked his fingers together for Farad. The little man placed his feet in Quamar's palms, almost slipping from the sludge. He gripped the giant's shoulder, saying a small prayer to Allah.

If the king attacked him before he could explain his presence, all would fail.

"Now," Farad whispered. Quamar lifted him, balancing the little man on his hands and shoved him up into the pipe. The boost put Farad halfway up the ten-foot tube. From there the thief used his back, feet and hands to leverage his way up the final few feet.

When he reached to top, he paused and listened. Secure in the fact that no movement came from the cell, Farad pushed the grate up with his head. "Your Highness," he whispered. "Don't hurt me, I am here to free you."

When he got no response, Farad paused, forcing his eyes to focus in the semidarkness.

The cell was no more than six feet square and totally bare. The king sat with his back to one corner. The metallic scent of blood permeated the air. Quickly, Farad scrambled out of the pipe, stopping dead.

Jarek had lost weight, his cheeks now sallow with fatigue and covered with three days' beard growth. His dark hair lay matted and sweaty against his forehead.

Farad's gaze dropped to the king's chest and bile rose to the thief's throat. Long slices of raw flesh tattooed Jarek's chest in wicked crisscrosses.

King Jarek raised his eyes to Farad's. The dark irises glowed on a hard, granite expression.

"Your Highness." Farad struggled to keep his voice low. "Master Quamar, he is down in the sewers. I am to tell you that he and his friends are going to release you soon. But first, I am to help unlock your chains."

Farad expected questions or rage, but the king didn't speak or move.

Fearful that Hassan and his son had broken Jarek's mind, driving him to madness, Farad kept up his whispering. If nothing else then to fill the eerie silence.

"Hassan has your wife and son. And Anna Cambridge. Quamar is here to help you save them." Sweat trickled down Farad's face as he worked the lock.

How much time had gone by? Farad knew he was babbling but the king said nothing, did nothing, while he worked on the cuffs. "Your son is a fine baby. I have seen him. Quamar and the princess have taken good care of him the last few days. Until Zahid came with his rebels—"

Suddenly, the cuffs broke free and Farad stood, expecting the king to follow.

When he didn't Farad grabbed his arm and pulled him up. "We must hurry. They will open the door soon. Your wife and son are alive and must be saved."

Jarek's gaze dropped to the little man. Growling, Jarek grabbed Farad by his throat and slammed him against the wall. With slow, deliberate fingers, he squeezed Farad's neck. "And why should I believe you?"

Chapter Nineteen

With his breath caught in his chest, Farad forced himself not to struggle. Fury stoked Jarek's black eyes, and instinctively Farad understood the king balanced on a thin line between hatred and madness.

"Please believe me, Your Highness," Farad gasped. "We must save your son. I must, if you won't." Jarek tightened his grip and lifted Farad off the ground. The thief grasped at Jarek's hands, trying to loosen them.

Quamar would be walking through the door soon, but Farad feared his life would end before then. "I have come to love your son as my own. Please believe me when I say I will do him no harm," Farad rasped in desperation. "He likes to pull hair, it makes him laugh. A high-pitched squeal that puts joy in those who hear it. He loves animals. And the princess—"

"Don't insult me."

"I beg your forgiveness, Your Highness. My only wish is to save Rashid from your uncle."

When Jarek jerked Farad higher, the thief's robes fell open. On his chest, whip marks stood out in bloody welts.

"Who did this?"

"Master Zahid. When I tried to stop him from taking Prince Rashid and the princess."

"The princess?"

"Anna Cambridge," Farad rasped out.

Jarek lowered Farad, then dropped his hand. The thief tilted his head back, sucked oxygen into his lungs.

Jarek tugged Farad's robes open, noting the damage matched his own. He glanced back up. "Where did you say Quamar was?"

The door swung in with a bang. "Right here, Your Highness." Quamar stepped over the guard's dead body without a second glance.

Roman stood sentry at the door, inclining his head slightly to watch Jarek out of his peripheral vision. He let out a long hiss.

Quamar's gaze swept over his cousin, but he managed to school his features. "Roman, Jarek needs a pair of pants," he said with forced casualness.

"No problem." Roman reached down to the

dead guard, stripped off his pants and tossed them to Jarek. "You can have his gun, too, if you want."

Jarek slipped on the pants and zipped them. "Yes, I want it," he replied, his voice deadly.

Roman checked the clip, then tossed him the pistol. Without a word, the three men left the room. Farad stood there, uncertain, until Jarek stopped, then turned back. The black eyes bore into Farad. "Are you coming?"

"Yes, Your Highness," Farad responded. He jumped over the dead guard and hurried out the door, unable to stop the smile that spread across his face.

For once, he was one of the good guys.

"WE'RE GOING TO have to split up." Ian eyed the small computer monitor in his hand. The men waited outside the main kitchen, watching for guards. Wherever there was food, there was a high probability of guards on breaks. And guards meant uniforms.

"Anyone ever suggest that you might have too many bloody rooms, Jarek?" Jordan muttered, his gun raised, his eyes focused on the nearby laundry room. "Hell, Windsor Castle is only half this size."

"I'm showing a lot of warm bodies still being held in some other areas of the palace. Mostly the underground levels," Ian murmured.

"If I had to guess," Cain said, keeping his voice low, "they haven't killed off all your loyal soldiers, Your Highness."

"Jordan and Ian, go with Cain, find the prisoners," Quamar said. "Release them, give them weapons from the guards that cross your path. And anything else they can get their hands on."

"Roman, Jarek and I will find Jarek's family and Anna," Quamar added. "Hassan is most likely holding them prisoner in the royal suites."

"Since there are twenty suites, we'd better get going," Jarek ordered, impatient.

"Farad," Quamar murmured. "You come with me."

"Master Quamar," Farad interrupted, eyeing the laundry chute near Jordan's shoulder. "I would prefer to move on my own. I can get into places you cannot."

Quamar glanced from the little man to the opening.

"I will not betray you," Farad added, "if that is what you are thinking."

"Actually, I was thinking of something else," Quamar answered. "Ian? Do you have any more of your transmitters?"

"Affirmative." Ian reached into his backpack and tossed Farad an earplug. "Take this, Farad. If you see them, let us know."

Farad smiled, placed the plug in his ear and opened the chute. "Yes, sir."

ZAHID ADVANCED ON ANNA, laughing when she scooted around the bed, placing it between the two of them.

When she glanced at the door, he laughed even harder. "You think Quamar is going to rush in through the door and save you?"

"Actually, yes," she said, stalling. "Or do I have to remind you what he's capable of?" Anna's back hit against the dresser. She put her hands behind her, searching for any kind of weapon.

"He's dead. And so is his father."

Zahid jumped across the bed and caught Anna by her bad wrist. When she cried out in pain, he smiled and tugged again. "Well, well. Seems I've caught a wounded dove."

Viciously, he twisted her arm behind her back.

Her scream echoed down the steel sides of the chute. Alerted, Farad eased himself out into the bathroom. Quietly, he opened the door no more than a crack.

Zahid had Anna pinned against the dresser with his back to the bathroom. "I usually go for slighter women, but you have amazing skin." He skimmed her cheek with the handle of his whip. "Soft as butter."

Noting the marble tile, Farad slipped off his shoes, then eased the door opened a few more inches.

Anna spotted Farad over Zahid's shoulder. The little man crept across the floor, his knife raised. "I usually go for more handsome men," Anna hissed, trying to distract him.

"That was a stupid thing to say—" Zahid glanced up, caught Farad's image in the mirror.

Zahid shoved Anna away and unraveled his whip. With a cry of warning, Anna grabbed Zahid's arm, stopping the whip mid-motion, throwing them both off balance.

Farad flung his knife, but missed Zahid. The blade hit the dresser and clattered to the floor.

"Bitch!" Zahid backhanded Anna. Pain exploded behind her eyes. She fell against the dresser, then to the floor. Out of her peripheral vision, she saw Zahid pull out his sword.

"No!" Anna scrambled to her feet.

But she was too late.

Farad yelled and dived for his knife. He hit the ground, rolled and came up with blade in hand.

Zahid whirled back and shoved his sword into Farad's stomach. Farad gasped, then moaned.

"Look what I have." Zahid shoved one more time, pushing the sword until the hilt embedded skin—bringing the men chest to chest. “A rat on a stick.”

“No!” Anna screamed.

“And I have a dead man standing,” Farad gasped. He raised his hand and shoved his blade into Zahid’s throat.

Zahid screamed, staggered back. He grasped at the knife. Blood flooded his throat, out his mouth, choking him.

Farad swayed, then grabbed the sword in both hands. With a cry of pain, he pulled the blade from his body and threw it aside.

“Farad.” Anna caught the little man as he slumped backward. With gentle hands, Anna placed his head in her lap.

“Is he dead?”

Anna didn’t look away from Farad. “Yes. He’s dead.”

“Don’t leave me,” he rasped, shutting his eyes against the pain.

“I won’t.” Anna’s throat constricted. “I promised. Remember?” Tears flooded her eyes, dripped onto his cheeks. “Please, God,” she whispered.

Farad opened his eyes, tried to raise his head. “Don’t, Princess.” Blood rattled in his chest, dripped from the sides of his mouth. “Please do not cry for me.”

"You saved me, Farad. I can't let you die," she whispered.

"It is too late, Princess," he rasped, his lips lifting into a weak smile. "I am a true hero, am I not?"

"Yes, yes you are." Anna's searched Farad's face through the blur of tears, willing him to stay alive. "You're my hero, Farad. And my friend." She brushed the hair from his forehead. "Always."

"Allah will welcome me, then, I think." He tried to nod, but couldn't finish.

"Yes, he will," she whispered, but knew he hadn't heard her. She gathered him closer, placed her cheek against his. "And if he doesn't…sneak in," she whispered.

"Anna?"

Quamar stood at the doorway, his gaze taking in the scene at a glance. With long, quick strides he crossed the room and crouched down beside her.

"He saved me." Anna's eyes found Quamar's, her tears blurring his features. "He died saving me."

"I know." Quamar gathered her close. "We have to go. You are not safe yet."

Anna nodded against Quamar's chest, then gently placed Farad back onto the floor.

"Once we secure the palace, we will take care of our friend. I promise, Anna."

Chapter Twenty

"Saree?" Jarek stood at the door, his feet spread, his gun pointing up.

"Jarek?" Saree glanced down at the torn pants, saw the blood, the wounds. "Jarek," she whispered. She shifted Rashid to her hip. "You're alive."

Jarek lowered the gun to his side and took a step forward. "I thought—"

"Jarek, no!" Anna barged through the doorway. Saree's eyes narrowed.

"Anna?" He took in Anna's blood-soaked clothes, then looked at Saree. "Why aren't you…"

Saree turned toward the desk. "I don't understand. Hassan had you tortured. But you look—"

"Jarek," Anna interrupted urgently. She glanced at the balcony, looking for Quamar. "It's not what you think. Saree—"

Saree swung around. In her hand, she held a

small revolver, its barrel pointed at Jarek. "Anna is about to inform you, darling, that I'm the one behind the rebellion."

Jarek stared at her; his fist tightened at his side.

"I could've gone through the whole act, but frankly I'm done with this and ready to move on," Saree said. "So we'll just take the shortcut here."

"Yes." The low, guttural word sliced the air between them. "Why don't we?"

"My, Zahid did a number on you, didn't he?" Saree shook her head. "The one thing I don't understand is why you didn't tell them what they wanted to know? You could have saved yourself a lot of pain, Jarek."

"Our son's life was at stake."

"So you thought I would be willing to sacrifice myself, too?" Saree shivered. "I'm maternal, darling, but probably not devoted enough to withstand torture." With a smile, she jiggled Rashid. Hearing his laughter, she said, "Good thing we don't have to test me, huh?"

"Who screamed in the cell next to mine?" he asked, emotionless.

"I don't know." Saree waved the gun slightly. "Some woman Zahid found. Does it matter? I'm sure she's dead."

Jarek's eyes flickered to Rashid. "Why?" But when he took a step forward, she raised her gun slightly. "No farther." Saree shifted her hip back, placing herself between Rashid and Jarek. "You would have settled. You would have made a deal with the United States, just because of some goodwill plan of yours. When there were a half-dozen other countries who would've paid twice as much for our oil."

"This is about money?" Jarek laughed, and the savagery in it made Anna flinch.

But Saree's lips tilted into a satisfied grin. "Darling, it has always been about the money. Why do you think I married you? My father might have been a diplomat, but he could no longer afford me."

Anna caught sight of Quamar through the balcony doors. He placed a finger to his lips.

"If you do as I say," Saree continued, "our son won't be hurt."

Quamar grabbed a tiled planter from the balcony and lifted it over his head.

"You would hurt our son?" Jarek asked, his voice hollowed with loathing.

The window shattered. Saree jumped back, caught sight of Quamar.

"Saree!" Jarek yelled her name like a curse. She swung back toward Jarek and fired.

Both guns exploded. Jarek staggered and dropped his pistol. Saree jerked. She looked down at her stomach, saw the blood form, spread. She dropped the pistol and went to her knees. "You shot me."

Anna ran and grabbed Rashid from Saree.

Saree tried to use the desk for leverage, but her legs buckled beneath her. Blood soaked her dress, turning it from ivory to crimson.

"Jarek," Saree whispered, then slid to the floor. "I…" Saree died mid-sentence, her hand stretched out to her husband.

Blood covered Jarek's shoulder, trickled down his arm, which hung useless against his side. But without glancing down, Jarek stepped over his wife's body and took Rashid from Anna.

He hugged his son, not caring that the baby screamed in his ear.

When Quamar joined them, Jarek asked, "How did you know?"

"Anna warned me on Farad's transmitter." Quamar pointed toward his ear. "You had a clear shot?"

"Rashid was on her back hip," Jarek acknowledged quietly. "I wouldn't have taken the risk otherwise."

Quamar nodded, understanding.

"And Farad?" Jarek asked Anna.

"He's dead," she whispered. Quamar gathered her close. "Saree left me with Zahid to…" Anna paused, took a deep breath, trying to get control of her grief. "Farad attacked Zahid and killed him. But not before Zahid stabbed him with a sword."

"Zahid is dead?" Hassan said from the doorway, pistol in hand.

"It's over, Hassan," Quamar answered. "As we speak, Bari's people and the United States Army are landing in Taer."

"Then I guess I have nothing to lose by shooting the three of you," Hassan responded as his eyes flickered to Saree's body and back. "I will not get a fair trial here."

"Instead..." Quamar moved away from Anna. "I will fight you. If you kill me, Jarek will swear you safe passage anywhere in the world." Quamar's eyes found Jarek's. The king was leaning hard now against the desk. He glanced at Quamar, gave a short nod of his head.

"I will take that deal," Hassan agreed. "Because when you die, your father will know I not only killed his son, but his wife, too. And went free."

"You killed Theresa Bazan?" Anna asked.

"I killed her and Jarek's parents. Actually, Saree should get credit for Makrad. After all, it was her idea." Hassan's smile was vicious when he turned toward Quamar. "You don't think I would let your mother live after your father turned his back on his country for her, do you?" He tsked.

"Then Jarek married Saree and she became pregnant. Well, everything seemed to fall into place."

"Not quite," Quamar responded, his voice tight.

"I want your word, Quamar. I win, I go free."

"So be it." But the fury was there, crowding him. He slapped it back. Killing was best done without emotion.

"And his." Hassan nodded toward the king.

"You have it," Jarek answered in a clipped tone.

Today might be Quamar's day to die, but his uncle would die first. Quamar did not take his eyes off Hassan. "Anna takes Rashid out of here."

"No." Hassan took a sword and a spiked club from above the fireplace. "She watched my son die. She can watch you die."

Quamar glanced at Anna. When she nodded, he stepped to the fireplace and grabbed a sword.

"Take two weapons, Quamar," Hassan jeered. "You'll need them."

Before Quamar answered, Hassan lunged at his back.

Anna screamed. Quamar swung around, blocked the blow. Steel clashed against steel.

"You might have strength on your side, Quamar—" Hassan backed up, then thrust, putting Quamar on the defensive, forcing him to block again "—but I have experience."

Quamar locked blades, then shoved back,

giving Hassan a taste of his power. "Come and get me, old man," he taunted.

Hassan growled and attacked. Quamar met him halfway, swinging his sword, catching, then deflecting, Hassan's blade in front of his chest.

Hassan backed up, circled his sword and his club, waiting for an opening. "I will win. And you will die."

Hassan lunged, but at the last moment, feinted left. Quamar moved but not fast enough to avoid Hassan's club. Pain exploded in his head. Razor-sharp lights burst behind his eyes. He stumbled back into the desk. His sword clattered to the floor.

Hassan laughed viciously, circling Quamar. "You think I didn't know about your injury?"

"This from a man who hid behind the skirt of a woman and her child. And still failed." Blood ran down Quamar's forehead, into his eyes. Quickly, he swiped it away and tried to focus through the blurred vision. "Like your son, you will not live to see the sunset. I swear to Allah."

Hassan screamed his rage and charged with both weapons raised.

At the last second, Quamar leaned into the attack, snagging his knife from his boot. Hassan saw the blade flash but couldn't stop his momentum. Quamar came up and in with his shoulder, sidestepping the sword. He blocked the club with his forearm and rammed the knife through Hassan's chest.

Hassan stopped, unable to move. Both weapons slid from his hands, hitting the floor. Quamar held the old man up by the knife, while disbelief etched Hassan's face.

"You lose." Quamar yanked the knife free.

Hassan collapsed to the floor, dead.

Chapter Twenty-One

A few weeks later

The night wind rustled the sides of the tent, sending a flutter over the walls. Anna turned down the lantern. It had been weeks since she'd seen him. She'd come to the desert to be close to him and been welcomed in with open arms by Bari.

"If you are listening, Farad, could you steal a miracle for me?"

She had tried staying at the palace but found herself looking toward the horizon. Wondering where he was. If he was suffering.

Anna slowly stripped off her robe, donned one of Quamar's shirts.

He'd left the night Saree died. The official version was that Saree, Hassan and Zahid had all died in the rebellion. At the hands of the Al Asheera. For Rashid's sake.

Anna moved to the pillows, lowered the netting. He'd left no note, no goodbye. Nothing.

After a week, Bari traveled back to his encampment. When Anna asked to go along, he smiled and pulled her into his arms. And she cried. She cried for Quamar, for herself and for those who died.

The silk felt cool against her skin. She lay against it and closed her eyes.

A hand slipped over her mouth. The fingers firm, tight. Anna screamed and started to struggle. Scratching at whatever she could hit.

A big body laid over hers, pinning her into the pillows. The weight of it familiar.

Quamar. Anna relaxed, tears pricking her eyes.

"Habbibi." Quamar removed his hand and slid his mouth over hers. The warmth of him took away her breath—and her anger. When he pulled back, he held her while she cried.

"You came back?"

"I had no choice. I left my heart here." He kissed her brow. "I would have been here sooner, except I went to the palace first. I thought you would fly home."

"I needed to be close to you. Here is close."

He nodded his head.

"How's Jarek?" Anna asked.

"Physically?" Quamar shrugged. "He'll recover quickly. But the other scars, the deeper ones… they will take some time."

"And support," Anna said, understanding. "To help him deal with the betrayal. And her death."

Quamar nodded. His gaze slid over her face.

"So does this mean you're going to have the surgery?"

"You know?"

"Your father told me the day we arrived here at his camp."

"Before our night together? And still you…" With a groan, he kissed her. "I should not have left you."

"Yes, I couldn't understand how you would rather die."

"If the consequences were just death, the surgery would have been done long ago. But to risk not being truly alive or dead was more than a risk I was willing to take."

"And now?"

"I could not stay away. I tried. For three days I cursed the Sahara. The heat. The wind. The solitude. I prowled the dunes, waiting for death. Always tormented by visions of long, blond hair, depthless blue eyes."

He brushed a tear from her cheek. "Even as the ache in my temples worsened, the pain did not compare to the heartache I suffered. I saw you in the bath, with a baby in hand, laughing, tickling, loving. The soft brush of your kiss against the curve of his cheek.

"I went to Maltri for peace and only found the loneliness. I turned around and came back. You were where I belonged." A pause. "Why did you come to see me at the hospital after your grandmother died?"

"I don't know. Impulse." Anna brushed away a few strands of hair, suddenly weary. "For some reason I had to meet you. My father told me what you had done. I wanted to see the man who had risked his life for my family," Anna reasoned. "Or maybe as a penance because of my mistake with Bobby."

"The kiss at the hospital?" Quamar asked after a moment. "Was it gratitude?"

"No." Anna shook her head. "You looked so alone. And I ached with loneliness. Somehow, something about you—I found familiar in me. I kissed you because I needed to. It started my healing. You gave me strength."

"That is why you were so angry with me in the tunnel."

"Yes, you were the last person on earth I wanted to hurt." With his silence came a rush of embarrassment. "I know it sounds stupid."

"No," Quamar said softly. "It was right. Because with me it was the same. The loneliness."

"I didn't understand," she said, her voice raw with unshed tears. "You risked your life for my family, for me when you didn't even know me. And now, when you love me…"

"Because the chances are I will neither be alive nor dead. And that I was not willing to accept." He leaned down, cupped her cheek and kissed her mouth gently. *"Roh albi wa hayati wa habibi."*

It took all his will not to make love to her. To cup her cheek in the palm of his hand, to feel for himself how real she might be.

"*Roh albi wa hayati wa habibi.*" Her voice flowed over him like sweet, cool water.

"Why are you here, Anna?"

"I needed to know something," she said softly.

"What?"

She raised her lips, brushed his once, twice.

At first he resisted, but he was a man dying from thirst. The third time they brushed, he groaned.

Unable to stop, his lips covered hers, diving deep into the recesses of her mouth, purging his loneliness, his heartache. Afraid she might pull away, he slipped his hand around the back of her neck, buried his fingers in her glorious hair.

When they broke free, his hands remained behind her neck, while his forehead tilted against hers. Her breath was quick, his own ragged with need.

He groaned again, this time deep in his chest. “I love you more than life itself. Even without this illness, I am nothing more than a shell of pain without you.”

“Serves you right,” Anna responded. “Do you think you’ve been the only one suffering? All those nights I lay in my bed wondering, is he in pain? Is tonight the last sunset he’ll see?”

She shifted away, only to be gathered closer, his arms tight bands around her. “I didn’t do this to us, Quamar. I didn’t send you away.”

His mouth closed over hers again, this time for forgiveness.

When he finally pulled away, he kissed her nose, her forehead. “I love you, Anna. A life with you is worth any risk.”

Her arms wound around his neck and her lips tilted into an impish grin. “The bigger they are…”

“Do not gloat,” he scolded, unable to contain his own grin.

Epilogue

The wind whistled through the cracks of the tent, causing Anna to stir. A hand slipped over her mouth, but before she could scream, weight pressed down on her, casually covering her from toes to chest, pushing her deeper into the silk and pillows.

"Hmm," the voice whispered wickedly in her ear. "What do I have here?"

The sound of his voice caused her to tremble. Tears slid down her temples. With aching gentleness he kissed them away.

"Still emotional?" His hand moved, but not before he trailed a fingertip across her lips.

"I'm sorry." Anna kissed Quamar's finger. "I didn't think I could ever be this happy."

"Do not be sorry, *Habbibi.*" His mouth covered hers in a sweet, healing kiss. "You cry with joy."

"I woke you because it's almost time," he

murmured, not wanting to disturb the quiet of the morning.

Fullness settled in her chest, making it heavy and tender to the light touch of his fingers. “I know—I can feel it.”

He gave her one last kiss, then stood. “I’ll be right back.”

Her husband walked naked to the bassinet a few feet away.

In the distance, a baby squealed and joy filled her. Until tears pricked behind her eyes once again.

They’d come to the desert to visit Bari. A short vacation before Quamar began his duties as Jarek’s advisor.

Quamar had survived the surgery. The recovery had been grueling, but a year later Quamar was back to full health. He had been lucky, Sandra said, in having lost only the peripheral vision in his right eye.

Considering the alternative, Anna thought, she considered them blessed.

Quamar knelt beside the bed and placed their son in her arms. The baby latched on, greedy for breakfast. Born with the thick, black hair of his father, the azure-blue eyes of his mother, he was her little warrior.

With a chuckle, Quamar eased himself behind

Anna until her back curled into his chest, enjoying the closeness while his son nursed.

It had become their ritual over the past four months, had started the day he'd been born. Quamar stole his finger over Anna's shoulder, smiling when his son grabbed hold with his small fist. "He's getting stronger."

"You say that every morning." But Anna whispered words of praise of love against the baby's cheek.

Kadan Farad Al Asadi. He was their miracle.

This time when the tears came, Anna didn't fight them. Instead, she whispered a prayer.

Thank you, little thief.

HARLEQUIN®
Next™

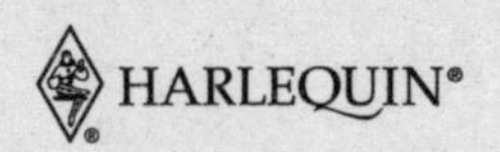

INTRIGUE®

COMING NEXT MONTH

#1017 RETURN OF THE WARRIOR by Rebecca York
43 Light Street
When the spirit of an ancient warrior takes over Luke McMillan's body, can Luke control his new urges long enough to save Sidney Weston's life—and free this trapped soul, *without* dying?

#1018 HIS NEW NANNY by Carla Cassidy
Amanda Rockport traveled to Louisiana to caretake for Sawyer Bennett's child, not expecting to discover a makeshift family that needed her to hold it together as their secrets pulled them apart.

#1019 TEXAS GUN SMOKE by Joanna Wayne
Four Brothers of Colts Run Cross
Jaclyn McGregor has a traumatic past she no longer remembers. But when ranching baron Bart Collingsworth rescues her from a car accident, he's not buying her story—but it won't stop him from getting mixed up with a woman who truly needs him.

#1020 IN THE DEAD OF NIGHT by Linda Castillo
Chief of Police Nick Tyson isn't the least bit happy to revisit the event that left his own family shattered. But there's no way Nick can turn the other cheek when someone tries to take Sara Douglas's life—even if he hoped he'd never see her again.

#1021 A FATHER'S SACRIFICE by Mallory Kane
Neurosurgeon Dylan Stryker will sacrifice anything, even his own life, to give his toddler son the ability to walk. But it will take FBI agent Natasha Rudolph to face her worst fear to save the man she's falling in love with and the little boy who has already captured her heart.

#1022 ROYAL HEIR by Alice Sharpe
William Chastain and Julia Sheridan lead a desperate hunt to rescue William's son—and restore his royal heritage.

www.eHarlequin.com

HICNM0907